Dreams of Being a Kiwi
A Novel by Paul Dore

Also by Paul Dore: *The Walking Man*.

Published by Paul Dore Creative Services. 1 Shaw Street, Suite 316, Toronto, Ontario, Canada, M6K 0A1, pauldore.com.
Book design by Paul Dore Creative Services.

Library and Archives Canada Cataloguing in Publication

Dore, Paul, 1978 - author
Dreams of Being a Kiwi / Paul Dore.

ISBN 978-1-9994067-0-7 (epub)
ISBN 978-1-9994067-1-4 (kindle)
ISBN 978-1-9994067-2-1 (pdf)
ISBN 978-1-9994067-3-8 (paperback)

For Phoenix

Chapter One

Something gnawed away at me on the inside that was not quite right.

Yet consistent.

Always there.

For a long time, nothing surfaced because everyone else was the same and I was completely healthy, although I grew to be suspect of the word healthy. From an outside perspective, there was no indication of anything awry. No signs that could be considered different than others. No undertow of darkness distancing myself from those around me.

Not yet, anyway. That comes later. Soon though!

School was not for me. Other kids were much further ahead in the development department. School didn't like me, I didn't fit in, had no friends. Lots of time on my own, it made no difference to me. A typical situation: the other kids made fun of me, called me crazy, and boy, in the way some people looked at it, they didn't know how right they were! The other kids were somewhat balanced - not especially cruel, just not kind.

My family moved a few times to a few different cities. They all formed together, the cities. All looked the same, those places. The kids in my classes always different, yet always the same. The outcast in every new situation, never made any real friends, never developed any real friendships. They never knew the real me, which in retrospect was probably a good thing.

The physical surroundings and my inside preoccupations never matched up, never felt like home. I did what was required of me - all my chores and school work. The key to harmony? Invisibility. I became the invisible boy. A genuine fear was to upset anyone. A word or action that drew a sideways glance with eyes full of pity, full of fear, full of disgrace.

My only friend was my older sister. She looked out for me, intimidated anyone that intimidated me. She walked with me to school, walked me back from school. We ate breakfast, lunch and dinner together. She was attentive to me, helped with my homework, gave me books to read. She had eight more years of experience than me on this earth. Always there when I needed her, there even when I didn't need her.

The closest thing I had to a real friendship ended badly. So poorly I wished it never happened. Wished I never knew this person. No names used to protect the guilty, but the memory a tattoo etched on the inside of my skull. That memory needed to be ripped out.

God knew I tried. God knew.

This boy talked to me one day in the hallway. One of the older popular kids whose kind never crossed the line over to my side. This just never happened! We hung out after school, walked to school, walked back from school. My sister left us alone, happy I had a friend.

Happiness never lasted.

Playing in the park where thick bushes lined the parameter. My friend suggested we hide in the bushes and ambush someone. Crawling through the bushes got us all scratched up. Crawled until we reached a small clearing in the middle of the bushes.

He had been there before.

The playing stopped, he looked at me funny. Asked if I wanted to play a different game, said I had to do everything he asked. I just wanted him to be my friend. He undid the button on my pants, pulled down my pants, an uncomfortable cloud spread from that area and encompassed my entire body. I knew not what to do. I knew not what this meant. How could I possibly have known what the implications were in allowing him to touch me? Afterward, I wrestled with the fact that I allowed him to touch me.

Allowed him.
Followed instructions.
The invisible boy.

Coming out of the bushes, I wanted only to never to see this friend again. The only friend I ever had. He told me not to tell anyone about what happened in those bushes. Swore to myself I'd die before I told anyone.

Darkness descended as I walked home alone. No appetite for dinner, no talking to anyone. Locked myself in the bathroom. Took a long bath, scrubbed every part of my body, double-scrubbed my pelvic area, lay down on my bed. My sister knocked on the door, came inside, knelt down beside my bed. Her eyes looked into my eyes and my eyes started crying. Impossible that any secrets were kept from my sister. She put her hand on my shoulder and I flinched. She only asked me one question, not more than one, promised never to ask me to tell her something that I did not want her to know. She asked: "Who was it?" Still no talking from me, only slightly shook my head. I never wanted this feeling. Wanted to sleep. Wanted these thoughts to leave.

Go away bad thoughts.

The next morning, my eyes opened and found my sister asleep on the floor beside me. She never left. She woke up when I touched her shoulder. Told her a name, she nodded her head.

That person never did anything like that again, not to me or anyone else. The message was clear: she told my friend that if he told anyone it was my sister that hurt him, there would be more trouble.

During those years, two specific experiences changed everything. In many ways, determined my life.

The first thing really blew up in our faces. My parents stopped talking to each other. We stopped eating together, did nothing together. My sister and I made our own family of two, my parents were just not interested in us. In some ways, I didn't blame them for anything. Was this kind of thing ever anyone's fault? They were not right for each other, not right for us. They just learned it too late. They had good intentions going in, but were good intentions ever enough? My sister and I dealt with it, carried on, kept calm, made our own lives away from them.

The second thing much more immediate, much scarier: the voice. Started the year I turned twelve, the year I was growing hair in new places, the time new thoughts came about myself and other people. The voice entered my head, not in a dramatic way, it was always there. Always a narrator speaking, dictating what was happening around me, commentating like a television sportscaster. Sounded like what I imagined my own voice sounded like. Nothing it said was necessarily untrue, just weird it was even there.

The problem came when this voice amplified, like it came from outside of my head. Whispered to me over my left shoulder. Whispered into my ear. I wondered if other people heard it, did other people have voices whispering in their ears? Tried to ignore it at first, but it just got louder the more I ignored it. Originally it was comforting. Thought the voice was on my side, that it had my best intentions in its heart. Looked out for me the way my sister looked out for me.

In the beginning, this outside voice did the same as the inside narrator. Commentated on the events that happened around me, only louder. Felt like watching my life on a television, never being directly involved in anything. Too afraid to be involved in anything. Wanting to be involved but scared, wondering if I had the right. When I talked with someone new, tried to do something I never did before, the voice grew louder. Critical of every move I made, upped the volume until I retreated, until I spoke to no one and never did anything new. The voice scared me, started to be there all the time, started to make suggestions about my actions. Tried to ignore these suggestions, but it came on stronger and stronger every day, becoming difficult to ignore.

Embarrassed, I hardly spoke. My sister was concerned and I knew she was trying to get my attention. Too far outside of me, too far away. The voice was close, right over my shoulder. It had the advantage. At first, it never asked me to do anything I didn't want to do. Soon it seemed anything I did, I did wrong. Anything I chose to do was the wrong thing to do. The voice started planting ideas in my head, started making bold and uncharacteristic suggestions.

I never blamed the voice for everything that happened to me. Definitely me that did all of those things. Me that set the actions in motion. The voice a guide, pushing me along. The ideas, the suggestions all seemed so real to me. All seemed like the right thing to do.

For the first time in my life, I truly believed in something unconditionally.

The ideas placed in my head became my own thoughts. The thoughts as real as anything else inside my brain. When a person touched a hot stove, got burned, they learned their lesson and never did it again. The voice dismantled this wire in my brain. The voice worked on my belief system. Planted those beliefs deep down inside, brought me into conflict with the outside world.

Several times a day I showered, believed being clean saved me from the bacteria circling in the air around me. Parts of my body scrubbed until red with irritation. Wore gloves in the summertime. The voice was good to me, congratulated me when I followed what it told me. The voice possessed a viciousness the times when I no longer listened. The voice would not let go so quickly and turned on me. Made other suggestions.

At fifteen years old I started a long journey into the darkest part of my life. Fell into a well of darkness, the walls slippery and unclimbable. Tried to numb the pain, stop the voice but it only came on stronger. Continually said I was not good enough, not strong enough, that I was weak. Stopped fighting it, gave into it when it started telling me to kill myself.

The transition occurred, there was a point where the voice seemed outside of myself, that it was talking to me like anyone else. It was so constant, so always there, that at some point I transferred over. The ideas the voice supplied become my ideas, I started to believe fiercely, as profoundly as when I fought it before. Yielded to it if only to stop the confusion, stop the fear. I unknowingly crossed over, became someone that worked in conjunction with the voice.

The tightness and the confusion actually went away, but only when I gave myself over entirely. A strange calmness came over me as I allowed it to take over completely.

At its mercy.

Very lost.

So lost.

Unrecognizable.

Nobody was home.

The invisible boy.

When the darkness totally surrounded my peripheral vision, only then, it felt right. The voice spoke over my left shoulder, whispered commentaries about my life and my decisions, chastising me as a sinner. During lunch hour at school, I stared at my lonely baloney sandwiched between two limp pieces of white bread. The voice was the strongest in quiet places like the library, like the washroom, like the long walk home when my sister could not accompany me.

A new girl named Mary sat down next to me in class. Desperate-looking and a fellow target of the various types of bullies. We became friends right away. Mary had all the signs of something not right at home - wore second-hand clothes, smiled a slight smile at inappropriate times. Her social cues were off. She was actually interested in school, thought it could take her places, could take her away. I walked Mary home at night to her small house. There was never anyone home. We did not talk very much, there was not much to talk about. What were we going to say? Me: "I hear voices that are increasingly getting out of control." Mary: "I have an unspeakable situation rumbling inside the paper thin walls of my house." What a fun conversation that would be!

We had comfort in each other's company. The voice did not like Mary, told me every day. Mary was my first defiance against its commentaries. The voice said things I could never have uttered with my own words: *Slut, her daddy crawls into her bed at night to tell her lullabies, weak, cries herself to sleep.* And on and on, sometimes I couldn't take it.

After a few weeks of silent walking to school and from school, Mary invited me inside her house. She wanted to pull back the curtain to show someone her life. I wasn't sure if that someone should be me. We went inside anyway, the inside dirtier than the outside. Plates piled high along the counters, bugs everywhere, mold spreading out from the ceiling corners. We toured her house, she showed me her room, closed the door, we sat on the floor.

We kissed clumsily. Our teeth clicked. Mary's saliva tasted of blood. We kept trying, her hands touched me, the voice screamed, *You are going to catch a disease.* The voice so loud the front door was not heard. We failed in hearing the steps approaching from down the hallway. The door thrust open. Mary's father, with the thickest neck I'd ever seen, grabbed me with one of his meaty paws, and literally threw me out the front door on to the porch. He stood in the doorway staring me down. I stared back, his stare was one of threat, mine was one of fear. I saw through a crack between him and the door, Mary stood behind him. She had tears in her eyes, she wanted me to do something, to stand up to him. The voice was too powerful, called me names, called me weak. I told it to shut up, spoke to it out loud. I never spoke out loud to it before. I called it names, swished around in a circle like a dog trying to catch its tail. Swore, shouted. I wanted it to leave. A light cloud of dust floated up around me. Stood up, stumbled down the steps, walked along the pathway to the street. Screamed out loud for it to stop, called it more names.

Then, blackness.

The next memory was waking up under a park bench a few blocks away from Mary's house. My mind silent, mouth dry with dust. Clothes dirty. Stood up, walked the rest of the way home, snuck into my bedroom, tears cleaned the dust off my cheeks while I slept.

The next day at school Mary did not appear. I never saw her again. I walked by her house, empty. When I stepped up to the porch, the voice grew louder with every step. I ran away - I was not running towards something, I was running away from something.

At the time I did not recognize that I had specific triggers, situations that flipped a switch, activating the voice. Mary's house was one such place. It was not the physical place, it was the kinetic energy that surrounded it, the experiences that haunted it. The energy fed off each other, connected to the mad energy inside my head, making it stronger, giving the voice power. People released all kinds of energy that, like ghosts, clung to the physical spaces I inhabited. Dangerous places are created by dangerous people. I became indirectly connected to these harmful environments by fate, not by choice.

After Mary, I succumbed to more of these negatively charged situations and environments. They were mostly the kind of places that I bought drugs, drank underage, sat beside other people burning themselves out. I had conversations with myself, no one noticed. They thought the drugs were strong. The drugs helped me fit in. I developed many superficial relationships that depended solely on the amount of drugs that were ingested, snorted, smoked. I went to parties, actually sometimes outgoing, sometimes just another person who tried to forget certain things about their life. The voice always lurked. The drugs were how I medicated myself, my attempt at dulling it into resignation. The drugs gave some relief, successfully dulled into quiet sabbaticals of submission. Soon, I realized the only way the voice would die, was if I died.

The voice was a parasite. I was the host that it manipulated, its only reason for existence was to torment. A lost soul that was murdered or cheated and karmically entered my mind. I was an excellent fit to push over the edge. Started believing it was god, at other times the devil. Marijuana dulled my mind, helped cope, forced the voice into dialogue with me in a relaxed way. When I was high, the voice forgot to criticize me, congratulated me on the downward spiral. We talked for hours, I took it into my confidence. I trusted the voice, told it everything when I was stoned. With the first toke, I knew that coming down would be the worst thing, that the voice came on stronger the soberer I got. It became loud, vibrated in my head, called me worthless, called me weak, called me pathetic.

The pot stopped working, the dialogue turned into arguments. I was thrown out of my dealer's basement, he told me not to come back. Shouting, screaming, arguing with nobody. Called me crazy. My drug dealer called me crazy.

Mushrooms messed me up, amplified the voice. No sleep for three days. During the highest point, I had a profound experience of becoming an enlightened being, only to be torn down into pieces, ending up on top of a building ready to throw myself off.

Ecstasy was next. The chemicals reworked the wiring in my brain, connected things that were not meant to be connected. Most of all, it confused the voice. I went to huge parties, got lost in the crowd, screamed, shouted and danced. The problem with ecstasy became apparent when I first came down. I did not want to kill myself, I only wanted to sleep for days, for months. All resolve disappeared through this drug. I gave into the voice; happily. It became liberation for me. I thought I could be saved if I just gave in. Walking down the street late one morning after a party, the drug slowly left my system. All of the people I walked by on the road started unveiling their masks. I saw their ugly, hideous real faces, the ones that smiled, the ones that showed everyone the falseness of the human spirit. The morning after a party was like the day after Halloween, when people undressed from their costumes, revealing the disgusting pigments of their true selves.

Ecstasy messed me up real good.

At first, I thrashed with the voice. The drugs gave me the energy to do so, but I soon became depleted and malnourished. One night I said the wrong thing to the voice and a large man thought I was talking to him. Out in the alleyway behind the club, he hit me again and again. Teeth popped out of place, blood vessels splattered, brain rattled.

It felt good.

I could have fought back, but I just lay unmoving among the garbage. He pummelled me enough. One person came out, pissed on me until I moved, startled him. He finished his piss somewhere else. I lay there until the sun came up. Sat up, felt my face - all the bumps, bruises, swelling. Tried to locate my teeth on the filthy pavement. The voice was quiet for once. Maybe the big man beat it out of me? That morning I was not wearing a mask, but people gawked anyway. They turned away fast, looked the other way, tried to ignore me, couldn't ignore me. I was too hideous, a reminder they didn't want to know about.

My sister found me passed out on my bed. Face stuck

to the sheets from the dried blood. She took me to the hospital, changed my bandages, did not ask me who it was or what happened. She knew that something was not right.

My physical wounds healed from that night except for a scar. The scar started at the corner of my mouth, on the left side, branched out and returned to itself on my chin. When I looked at myself in the mirror for years to come, I saw that scar, looked inside it, scratched it, stared, waited to see if anything came out.

After the alleyway and in the days that followed, a calmness came over me in the form of the voice. It whispered non-stop, conjured a light white dust around my eyes that I felt surrounded my body. I stared through the window of my bedroom, looked to the sky, something outside spoke to me, cobwebs fell away from my mind.

Unbeknownst to me, my family was completely falling apart. My sister attempted to hold it together. She failed miserably, it would be the only thing she failed at. To her, it was everything, she never got over it. This failure was what committed her to me, when everyone left, when all was gone.

My father simply left, he did not ever take an interest, even when I was somewhat developing normally. I couldn't remember three conversations I had with him. He left, it was not a big deal to me. He woke up one morning, ate breakfast in silence, avoided my mother, prepared for work, left for work and never appeared at work. His car was found abandoned in the next city, no signs were ever seen again. When he didn't come home that night, my mother waited for him. My sister knew he was gone. My sister was twenty, went out the next day, got a job in a pizzeria. She told me how hot it was in the pizzeria. She operated the oven, put a pizza in the oven, took it out. Over and over again. She stood eight hours every day after she was done school in front of that oven.

My mother died soon after in an accident. My sister knew it was suicide. There were no other cars on the road. She slid off a highway on-ramp, crashed three stories below. It was a road she never drove on. The police at the scene blamed the slick roads from rain earlier in the day. My sister scuffed. She knew the truth, she didn't say anything to contradict the report.

We stayed in the house. My sister became my guardian. We slipped through the cracks. She kept going to school, stood in front of that pizza oven. When she came home, her skin was hot to touch, face sunburned from being inside all night. If it was another person, I could've recognized the tiredness in her eyes. Life can rundown a twenty-year-old with such burdens. Not my sister. She had an unending source of energy, never gave up, always helped me.

I was left alone a lot. I could not blame my sister, she had the responsibility to support us. Further down the well I went. My journey into darkness moving at an alarming rate. The dissension was disguised in the form of a white light. Most days I lay on my bed atop crumpled sheets looking into the face of God. I believed

I saw the light. The voice described all of the majestical things I must do to placate this God, to service him, provide him with reasons to save a spot for me in heaven.

I fell to my knees, slamming the floor with my fists over and over, until bloody. Pushed tears from my eyes, felt less than a person, inhuman, as though I was encased in a glass box. If someone talked to me, I assumed they were finding fault with me inside their mind. If someone looked at me in the subway, they formed a harsh judgment. I banged on this glass box, wanted out, but I was also scared – if the glass was shattered, I had no idea what was beyond it or what I would do with my new found freedom.

Those days in my room alone, I fell to my knees in repentance - wanted to be forgiven, but I knew that forgiveness came with punishment. This vengeful God made it understood how you crossed him. I took my shirt off, unlooped my belt, whipped my back again and again. The leather was cold, did not hurt. With each swipe, I felt him smiling. I knew this was what he wanted and I was determined to devote my life to him. He was the way, for the voice told me so.

My sister visited me in the early mornings between work and school. She knew I was sick, knew the illness I had been fighting had taken over my body, wrecking havoc. She did not know what to do. It was not her fault that she thought it would pass. It was not her fault she thought I just needed time to heal. I started going out everyday wearing sandals, a white robe, my hair growing fast, knotting into curls, prickly facial hair covering half my face. I did not wash, walked the streets, screamed at the top of my lungs. I went to areas the voice told me to go, went to places in the city where rich people resided, marched down the centre of the street with my arms extended, pointing towards the sky. I screamed, shouted, yelled God's words, wanted the world to know that He knew we were all going to hell and we must join him, punish ourselves, punish each other to find ourselves again, purge the evilness that existed in our souls. Marched all day, all night and I returned home, crawled into bed for my sister's morning visit.

I was not fooling anyone.

God's will on my side, he protected me. When it was my time and the gates opened, I would be welcomed. This was not the case, this would never be the case. The voice sold me on it, the voice whispered more, the whispers turned into yells, louder and louder. I was at its mercy, would do anything. No resemblance of my past self was evident, even my face hid behind long stringy hair, behind an unkempt beard, food crumbs locked in its curls.

A pressure behind my eyes formulated. It was never enough, could never satisfy Him. I got down on my knees every day and asked Him to forgive me. Asked Him for help, a sign. I washed the feet of homeless people, visited churches, screamed to the heavens, had conversations about Abraham with the voice. The voice or god, I couldn't remember which, told me I needed to sacrifice something, needed to make something that was alive dead. Needed to turn it inside out, needed to hold its still-beating heart in my hands.

The neighbour's cat was always in our backyard. It was afraid of me before and had good reason. I caught the cat, removed the knife I took from the kitchen, tied the cat down, placed the tip at its neck. The cat looked at me in the eyes with its yellow eyes. The eyes looked human. I saw fear in those eyes and I could not hurt the cat. Instead, I took the knife to the tip of my finger, punctured a small hole. Red blood dripped. Licked it, brought the knife down to my wrist, stared at the knife, saw my reflection in the blade.

The cat wiggled free of its restraints, ran away. When far enough, it stopped, looked at me. The cat spoke, it said, "What do you want to ask me?" I asked, "What do you want from me?" The cat smiled, replied, "Remember to floss after dinner." I blinked twice, I asked, "Is that it?" The cat meowed, ran away and I dropped the knife, collapsed on the ground. My sister found me there in a heap, in the fetal position, not knowing what my name was, I knew nothing except I was done with Him.

Completely irrational, I didn't recognize my sister. I thought she was messing with me, thought she was from another planet, thought she was going to hurt me. In the end, I only hurt her. She no longer saw her brother in my eyes, she saw someone else, someone vacant.

I lay in bed all day, never slept, sometimes cackled

hysterically, sometimes weeping uncontrollably. When I did get up, I walked for hours with no destination, talked to no one. I thought they were all part of a system that was created to crush my soul. Whenever I went out for a walk, it seemed to rain. I thought if He was up there, He was sending me signals, telling me my life was not worth living. Lights followed me around. Out of the corner of my eyes, I heard people talking about me and when I looked at them, they went silent, not wanting me to know it was them.

I determined that everyone experiences the world in their own way, that everyone had a perception of every living thing and how they interacted with it. People were guardians of their own environment. Some of us thrived, some of us created worlds where success and companionship were found. My world was constructed out of misery. I understood this as I sat on a park bench, staring at the cracked concrete for hours without a thought in my head. I became a blank page, nothing new was being written, and the past was being washed away in the rain until it was illegible.

Even the voice seemed to abandon me. I figured its job was done, there was nothing more to torment. My mind was stillborn. Did not move forward, did not remember. The only persistent thought was how to end it all.

I learned later that after the incident with the cat and the knife, my sister had begun to take steps to have me sectioned to a hospital. She researched the proper steps, filled out the proper forms, went before a judge to get an order to arrest me. I had become a danger to myself, the papers said I might hurt someone and needed to be hidden from view. I looked back with enormous guilt over what I put my sister through - the names I called her, the blame I shifted from me to her, from my parents to her. She knew where it was coming from, she had patience, she was determined I would get better.

I wanted to free myself from this disaster of a life. I ran a bath of cold water, dumped ice in the bath, set the razors on the edge of the tub, removed my clothes, stepped into the bath. It was cold, so cold I barely felt it. I rested my head on the side of the tub, my head was so tired. I would finally end it here, talked myself into believing I was doing this for my sister. One more thing to put on her. I was removing the burden of taking care of me, of staying up late wondering what she would find when she came home. She could stop worrying about it, could move on with her life, construct her own world, start over, start a family, find what she deserved.

The voice had come back over the last few days, it was screaming at me. It was not angry, it was happy, complimentary towards me. I was finally doing something with my life, finally giving it what it wanted from me. I moved slow, stared at the ice melting around me, looked at the razor blades, my reflection shone in them. I took the blade in my hand, felt disconnected from where I was, from what I had become. My salvation felt heavy in my hand, I placed it against my wrist, made an incision like a doctor.

Red.

From here I floated on a breeze, disappeared, the voice was my only companion. I shut myself out from the world, completed a journey that commenced years earlier. I fell into red-hued darkness that would take me further years to wake from. My body ceased to exist, I traveled the earth, flew in the atmosphere, along shores of places I wanted to visit when I was a kid, walked on beaches, climbed trees, looked down from mountaintops.

Everywhere and nowhere.

At one point, I visited my family before I was born, saw my mother holding my sister. I saw my father arriving home from work. They were happy. It was only until I entered their lives that everything began to crumble. I was a symbol of everything that was wrong with their pasts, a symbol of what the future had in store for them.

It was all my fault.

I was taken away from them, flew up towards the Arctic circle, thrust into a cave, the cave was cold, dark. I was alone - where I deserved to be. I felt there was still not enough room between the people of the world and me, so I burrowed deeper into that hole. I slept when I was tired, I did not need to eat, when I was far enough, when it was dark enough, I curled up, hoped to be taken away, to be left alone so I could leave others alone. To live, not to die. To live out my years in hibernation, never again among people, but to be alive to pay for my sins.

Chapter Two

My sister found me in the bathroom, in the tub, bleeding from one wrist, shivering from the water. The ice had melted, the cut was not deep. The blood more symbolic than anything else. I had passed out for a while, but conscious when she walked in. She did not look surprised, only nodded her head. Her mouth went straight, not a frown, not a smile, and she did not rush to help me. She just stood there for a while. We looked at each other. Later she told me my eyes said, *Help! I need you like never before.* For the first time in her life, she was frozen.

She helped me out of the tub, I did not want her to

touch me. I screamed and shouted, but she persisted. She lay me on the floor, my body shrivelled up into a ball of shivers. I could not look at her. The voice was in full swing, told me my sister was going to kill me, told me I should be afraid of her, told me I should cut her with the razor blade. I could not listen to the voice anymore, could not move. I stared at the underside of the toilet bowl.

The concept of time evaporated. My sister stroked the hair from my face. In my head, I told her to stop, screamed it loud, but it came out as barely a whimper. I tried to cry, no tears came, I was okay with that, I didn't want my sister seeing me cry.

After more time, two cops entered the bathroom. Large men, both had shaved heads. One bald, the other had tiny sprouts of hair - he buzzed it for the style. Chests like tanks, the typical blue uniforms, guns at their sides. I wanted to reach for one. They wore thin latex gloves. I thought I was dreaming until they grabbed me. My sister yelled at them to be gentle, I was not going to hurt them. They both snickered at the same time, how could they know for sure? They tried to grab me again. Strength came into my joints when I realized they were here to take me away. I swung my arm around but was too slow. The closer one moved out of the way, the other grabbed my arm, twisted it, turned me around, bent my arm in a way it shouldn't bend. Yelled in pain, struggled in his grip, but he was too strong.

The officers picked me up, any remaining energy

drained out of me. My sister was standing in the doorway, the policeman said, "Excuse us." She just stood there, staring at me, watched as they walked me out of the bathroom each holding on to one of my arms. They brushed by my sister and walked me through the front door.

Outside the sun was bright, much too bright. My legs went limp, the policemen caught me. My sister stood watching from the door, she said she would follow me to the hospital, said she would be there at every step, said she was sorry, she had no other choice, she wished there was another choice. I wished she stopped. I never saw my sister pleading with anyone and didn't want her to start with me. Looking over my shoulder, I tried to tell her to stop, but when I turned around the voice told me not to say anything, so I just glared at her. There was no strength for anything else.

The policeman put a hand on my head, guided it into the car. That was nice of him. When all inside, I asked, "Where are we going?" The officer in the passenger seat replied, "The hospital." I asked, "Does everyone get a police escort to the hospital to fix their cut hand?" No answer. The backseat was enormous, the seats black leather, a tangy smell.

I tried to put the window down, but it didn't work. The automatic windows must have been broken. I told the officers this, thanked me for letting them know. I asked, "Okay, really, what's the deal?" They responded, "We are taking you to the hospital for people with a mental illness." I said, "We are going to the wrong hospital. There is nothing wrong with me mentally, it is my wrist that is cut." They said, "Exactly."

This was all the voice talking for me. The voice had taken over completely, I was no longer in control. It was fighting for freedom, perhaps also scared. It knew where I was going even if I didn't.

I asked them to open the window. The driver opened it a crack, a crack was enough. Breathed in the air, replaced the stale air of the car with fresh air. Inhaling too quickly, my chest tightened, I slumped back in the seat. Out the window, little kids walked with other little kids, tiny backpacks bumbling up and down. As they walked, they laughed. People waited for stoplights to change at street corners. Someone was dressed up as a giant apple advertising Apple Car Wash, waving at the cars, trying to encourage them to use his car wash. I tried to wave at him, but he did not wave back.

The car turned into a parking lot beside a giant building. We pulled into the back. They brought you in through the back, so the people entering the front for visits did not see those being dragged in by the police. Must have been terrible to be one of those crazy people dragged in through the back. The car parked, engines cut, a noise vibrated under the hood. The policemen did not move, both their eyes were on me. They asked, "Do you know what this place is?" I replied, "The crazy house where they bring crazy people. Why did we go to this hospital? It's my hand that is cut, not my mind." They both nodded their heads, got out of the car, opened the door for me, helped me out of the car. My sister pulled into the lot, I did not want to see her right now.

Automatic doors made a hydraulic noise as they parted horizontally for us. We approached the front desk, a young woman sat reading some files. The policemen got her attention, she looked up, they spoke, I heard not what they said. The sound was turned off. Her name tag said Helen. Two men almost as large as the policemen came walking down the hall. Dressed in all white. They took my arms, thanked the policemen. Before the policemen left, they padded me on the shoulder, gave me a fake smile, left the building. Doors slid open, slid closed.

The two men in white said their names were Larry and Harry. I didn't know who was who. They walked me down the hallway, we entered a room, they shoved me on to a chair. The room was decorated nicely, another chair beside me, a desk before me. Bookshelves with large books, several photographs of one family, a window the length of the wall behind the desk. If this were my office, the desk would face the window.

The door opened, my sister entered, I told her to go away. She didn't listen, sat in the chair next to me. She said nothing, I now know she didn't know what to say. This was much more of a nightmare for her than for me. She knew exactly what all this meant, I had no idea.

An older man entered I recognized from some of the photographs spread around the desk. Head down in a file. He sat behind the desk, flipped a page. My sister was getting mad, I knew the look. Not the kind of doctor that would fix my cut wrist, one that would try to fix my cut mind. No head medicine would heal me the way a cut was stitched up or a cast was put on. He had a big job with me. The doctor had silver hair, wore round glasses that reached the edge of his nose, the glasses looked like they were going to fall off. Tired lines around his eyes. A mouth so big I might be able to put my entire fist into it. His ears stuck out east and west and he wore a thin black tie over a blue striped shirt under the white coat.

The voice was quiet, seemed scared of this man in the white coat. The voice was biding its time, assessing the situation. Drained from all its screaming, glad it had decided to take a break.

The doctor finally looked up, asked my sister some questions. I could not hear what they said. The wiring had been cut in my brain that translated what people said. They might as well been talking in another language. The doctor turned to me, spoke, it came out as English, "How are you feeling?" I said, "I feel fine. Why am I sitting here? Why am I not getting my wrist tended to? This is a hospital, isn't it?" The good doctor smiled, said, "This is a psychiatric hospital. Your sister filed the necessary paperwork to get a court order to have the police escort you to us. We believe you are suffering and want to help you." I said, "You must have me mixed up with someone else." The doctor responded, "No, this is the truth, this is the reality. We only deal in truth and reality here. You and your sister are two very courageous people. This is a difficult time." I said, "Damn right, I know what you're talking about." I turned to my sister, "Can we leave now?" Her quiet eyes broke my heart.

Something snapped inside my head, I started to cry. I wanted to leave, I wanted to go away, I was not crazy. Sure, there are some problems, but they're my problems, I didn't need to share them with anyone. I wanted to go, stood, I said to my sister, "Let's go, we don't have to listen to these people, this man, with the white coat, he is clearly the crazy one, not me, I am perfectly okay. I nicked myself with the razor while shaving, that's all. Now I will be strapped into a bed unable to make my own decisions, dying inside - kill me now, that's what I say. If I was an animal that was crazy, shoot me, put me out of my misery, you bastard son of a bitch mother fucker. Why bring me here? You should have just taken me out back, shot me dead, thrown me in a ditch."

Slumped in my seat exhausted, drained. I never spoke to my sister like that. She did not reply, just took a large breath, sucked air in through her nostrils, turned to the doctor. They looked into each other's eyes, my sister nodded her head quickly three times while looking down at her feet. She felt me staring. Something was happening outside of my control.

Larry and Harry grabbed me from behind, pulled me up and over the back of the chair. We left the office, left my sister, I yelled, "I'm sorry! I'm sorry! Bring me back! Let me go!" My feet went limp. They dragged me down the hallway, unlocked a door, we entered a room.

This would be my room for the next few years until I transferred to another wing. The room was all white, a sheet separating the room down the middle. There were two beds, one on either side of the sheet, no one else was here, they lay me down on one of the beds. I couldn't move, I didn't move, they said they would be near if I needed anything.

Paralyzed except for the ability to move my head. Looked to my right side, a window. A bright light shone through the window, the bright light blinded my eyes. The voice quiet, my mind shut off, all wires cut. My soul escaped, I fell into blackness, a blackness so deep, a void so wide. Gone, I wanted to die, I did not have enough energy to die. My mind left my body through my ears, it floated away above me. Gone, gone, gone into blackness. Blackness surrounded me, blackness entered my heart, everything went black.

Woke up. At least I thought I woke. Opened my eyes, could not see. Only the blackness, blacker than black. Felt as though I was lying down, felt a bed or mattress below me, I lay on my side with my eyes open, saw my body but nothing else, only the blackness. In the blackness, my body did not move. I could not make it move. Commanded it, nothing moved.

Closed my eyes, saw my body floating. Moved my left arm, it waved back and it waved forth in front of my face. My sight was blurry. I opened my eyes, my arm had not moved. I was paralyzed, felt my arm moving, but in reality, hadn't moved. I closed my eyes again, once more the arm moved, I popped my eyes open, nothing.

My heart raced, moved fast, too fast. A heart attack? All my pulses - the ones in my neck, on my wrist - all pulsated loud. Kept my eyes opened.

Every once in a while, the doctor joined me in my darkness. A nurse I remembered as Helen entered, they always looked at me with eyes I did not like. They got sucked back out of my darkness.

No sign of my sister.

The voice soothed me, cooed over my shoulder, whispered I would be alright. *Just stay here, they will let you go, we will get out of this.* The voice was already planning. I tried to ignore it, but it was all I had. It was the only thing that talked to me in the darkness. The voice spoke to me, reminded me who I was laying on that bed.

Hours passed, days. The darkness receded, soon I saw the bed beneath me. After that, the floor appeared. I fell asleep, woke up to a visual orchestra of the window showing me outside, reminding me that I had not died, there was a world I might return to. Clouds moved slow across the sky, one of them took the shape of what the voice looked like. The clouds fluffy with many layers, the centre a greyness, an area that you could not see through, that held the potential of danger. The rest of the room materialized, started to move my arms with my eyes open. Rolled over on my back, stared at the ceiling.

Helen had a relaxing voice. The doctor had a voice that was difficult to take in. The first time I sat up, my head spun. How long I had been laying there? The voice told me two weeks. I did not believe, could not accept. Placed my feet on the ground. The doctor came in, told me to take it easy. I ignored him, he went to help me, I screamed, shouted, yelled for him not to touch me. I stood up to defend myself, stood too fast. Tumbled to the ground, hit my head on the side of a side table, felt blood. A return to the blackness. Before I passed out, the voice said, *That's what you get.*

I had enough of all this laying down. Stood up slowly this time. Tied the back of the hospital gown. My wrist was bandaged, there was a dull pain. Walked around my bed, a bed where nightmares filled my days, my nights. I didn't remember any at that moment, barely knew my name. The only thing that existed was that damn bed. Staring straight ahead, I focused on the door, wanted out, needed air, my feet would not move. Willing them to move, I tried to pick one up with my hands. They were cemented into the ground. Stopped, closed my eyes, breathe. Commanded my right foot to move, my left foot moved. Not every battle was mine to win. Right foot followed, they worked on their own. We made it to the doorway.

Down the hallway, there were several doors. A door at the end of the hall said EXIT. I used the wall for support, it took ten hours to get there. Finally pushed the door open, took all my strength. Through the door, there were stairs, damn it. One stair at a time. I almost fell several times, made it to the bottom, there was nowhere to go except for a sign that said EMERGENCY

EXIT - ALARM WILL SOUND IF DOOR OPENED. I opened that door anyway, I didn't care. No alarm went off, well, no alarm I heard. The air filled my lungs, I lost all control, fell to the ground. There was grass, I crawled to the grass, lay on the grass. My face rested, it was cool, smelled like dirt. I fell asleep. They found me. When I woke, I was back in my bed.

In and out of consciousness.

When I woke, nothing except blackness. Sometimes I was hyper-aware of the cracks in the ceiling, someone breathing on the other side of the curtain, the feeling of the mattress under me, the wind rustling outside.

The doctor entered the frame, I yelled. After a few of these episodes, I saw him no more for a long time. Helen took care of me, looked at me the way I wanted someone to look at me. She did not ask questions I could not answer. I was in a deep dark hole.

One morning or day or night I opened my eyes, my sister sat in a chair beside the window. She was looking at me, asked if I recognized her, I said, "Of course." She moved her chair closer, the chair legs scratched along the floor. Before the darkness, I never recognized her features: the hair perfectly pulled back, the arc of her eyebrows. When she settled back in the chair, she smiled a warm smile, there was something familiar and comforting in her smile. She spoke for a long time.

"I am sorry for all of this," she said. "Maybe at some point, you will recognize it as a necessity to save yourself from yourself? Maybe you will be eternally upset with me? I don't know, doesn't really matter to me. What does matter is you know I did this because I love you. They told me not to say much, to listen if you had something to say, to agree to be comforting and supportive. That all goes without saying, but what I will not do is talk down to you, talk to you as though you are a child unaware of what is happening to you. I regard this as pointless and condescending. You are a person, a grown-up, someone that is ill, but someone that needs to learn who they are again. To be acquainted with the individual you have been separated from and this can only be accomplished by talking to you like you are my brother and understanding that any words that come from my mouth are out of love whether you want to hear them or not.

"You are a brave person, braver than I am. For a long time, I ignored your problems, figured they would go away, convinced myself it was because our father was an asshole and our mother was a lost soul. That perhaps you believed you were like them, that you needed to act out in ways that complemented their behaviour for you to have a better understanding of your life. I will tell you the truth. I know this is not the best time to have this conversation, that we had many other opportunities, but I don't want to waste any more time.

"Your father was a fool. He had a beautiful wife, he had two wonderful children and he threw it all away. He drank and was violent and he disappeared out of our lives. I will tell you about your mother. She was a sad soul, unable to cope, she suffered her whole life in silence. First through an overbearing father, one that shunned her existence, then through a husband that cheated, lied, stole, but worst of all, held her captive within the confines of her own life. Held her captive in a box, a kind of glass box where she only knew she was alive by the fog left on the glass by her breath. She loved you, she loved me. The official report was her car flipped off the road and she died an accidental death. But you know and I know this was not the truth. I want to say it out loud, so it becomes a truth that we acknowledge, or at least consider. Maybe if we agree to it together, wherever she is, she will rest a little easier to know that we know the mystery is gone and we understand. And we remember the truth. What do you think about that?"

My head nodded, I had tears in my eyes, I let them fall.

"You became my responsibility," my sister continued. "I lied and bribed certain people so we could be left alone. The world was going to stop moving on its axis before you and I were separated. I realize now I made a mistake, but people make mistakes, that is in our DNA. Especially ours. It is inevitable, please do not think I forgive myself, please do not think I am shifting blame to other people or other circumstances. I firmly blame myself. We will both make mistakes in the future, maybe I am making one right now? I have always tried to make the right decision for both of us.

"I was not around, I was working too much, trying to help us get by. I wanted, was determined for us to thrive, for us to prosper in all the ways our full family could not. I wanted to prove that we were survivors. I understand now that this was more for me than for both of us. I regret that. I do not think regretting is terrible, it is just a way to not repeat certain mistakes. In a way, all that work paid off. I never told you any of this, never thought you needed to know.

"I started at that pizzeria, I met some people. That damn oven, my own life disappearing one drop of sweat at a time. Muscling my way into other places, I met some people. They liked me, I cannot say I liked them. Impressions were made, I started working, I am still working. I am making money, more than enough money to take care of both of us for the rest of our lives. I hope you understand, I don't want to go any further on that at the moment. I also understand that money is not what will make you better. It can make you more comfortable, but it is you and me that will help you get better.

"I admire you. I am sorry. I would have crumbled a long time ago under the pressure you have been under. I have been learning about your illness. It is not a physical ailment, it is not something you can take medicine for and it will automatically heal. I am afraid for you. This is very serious, but you will get better because I know you. Sometimes you might not be recognizable but deep down inside there is still the part that is you, that wants to get out, that wants to be free.

"I had you arrested, sort of. I went behind your back, went through the proper channels, researched what my options were for you. I want you to understand that I am not dumping you here for someone else to solve the problem. You are not a problem to solve. I am here for whatever you need. Please nod your head if you understand this but only if you truly understand this."

My head nodded. I wanted her to stop talking but didn't want her to stop talking.

"When a person is mentally ill, they may become a danger to themselves or to others, so you can file papers with a special court where they determine whether you should be brought into the hospital and through what means. There was a hearing where we discussed your case with a judge. The only way to get you here would be through an escort, which meant I had to get a court order. The judge agreed, the papers were signed, the deal was sealed, the date arranged.

"I want to tell you how difficult this was for me. I am not telling you so you will have sympathy for me. This was out of love, I did this because you are all I have. I did this because I knew something was very wrong with you, but I don't know about such things. I needed help and I only wanted the best for you, to do things in the proper way to minimize my mistakes.

"I knew you were taking drugs, I thought you were just experimenting. Don't ask me how, I just did. But your behaviour, I did not understand. You talked to yourself, talked to other people. Loudly, softly, yelling sometimes. Things were out of control, I was not around for you, I was not there for you. I know what I said earlier about regrets but I deeply regret this.

"The day was scheduled for the police to arrive. This happened to coincide with your attempt at suicide. When I walked into that bathroom, saw the blood, the air left my lungs, my mind went blank. I thought you were dead. I tried to imagine my life without you, all I saw was a blackness. There is no me without you. My reasons for living did not seem to run parallel with this image. I could not comprehend this concept. I would trade my life to reverse our roles. You were still breathing, you were still here. The blank area in my brain filled up with images of you, I almost suffocated as my mistakes and my ignorance of the situation over the past few years flooded my system. But you were still alive. We realized it was not a bad cut, you just passed out. We put you on the floor, you felt like a rag doll, the life was being sucked out of you.

"Somehow I was determined to help you find yourself. The police took you away. I followed them in my car - that was the longest drive of my life. I wanted to take you away from all of this. Arguing with myself, I wondered if I should join you in the hospital, pull up a bed right next to you, but I knew that this was the right decision. We sat in that office, I must admit I was going to lose my shit. I tried to keep myself calm. In my line of work, my calmness has been my biggest asset. They pulled you away, I followed them out into the hallway. They pulled you away from me. I stood there unmoving long after you had disappeared from the hall. I couldn't move, didn't know what to do except that I wanted to crack the heads of the police and kill those orderlies.

My work turned me into someone that gets what they want. I wanted to hurt them, but I stopped myself. The only thing that has kept me going is thinking of you. I sat at home, miserable, unable to hold a thought in my head, wondering if you were alright.

"Then yesterday a thought took hold in my head, it just sat itself down, erased all the other thoughts. The thought was that you are a strong person. It started small, that thought, but it grew, it grew fast, took over, made me strong. Your strength reached from this bed over to our house, it said to go see you. Even though they told me to stay away for a while, the strength told me I needed to explain some things to you, no matter what state you were in. It told me that you have been strong for the both of us, that it is you that has been struggling all these years alone with no one listening, no one realizing what was happening. That you had lived for so long with all these things in your head, but you kept going, kept fighting, scrapping it out with yourself. You were not going to give up, you were fighting for something. I realized you were fighting for something that most people have no concept of - you were fighting for yourself, for your mind, your sanity, you were doing a balancing act to find yourself. You needed to find the core of who you were to heal yourself, even though you probably did not know you were sick.

"I am here to tell you that you are not alone, that I love you no matter what has happened, no matter what has been said, no matter what will happen. I want you to know that you are loved, that we are brother and sister, the same blood flows in our veins, we are together in this and I am nothing without you. I have been reading about what you have seen, what is going on in your head. You must feel very alone, but I want you to try and understand - maybe you will not understand this right now but soon come to understand - that I stand beside you. Together we are strong, that there hidden inside of you is the strength to change, to grab hold of yourself, to move forward, to heal yourself. I know the strength is inside you, I can see it, I just hope you can see it as well. That is enough for now, some of these things I say are difficult. I hope you are taking this all in, that you are feeling the strength inside as I feel it. I will leave now, you need more sleep, so sleep, close your eyes, remember my voice, remember it is here for you, it means you no harm, only help, only support, only to aid in you making yourself better. Good night, my brother. I love you with all my heart. With all my heart."

Chapter Three

Little by little, I remained conscious for more extended periods of time. I did not get out of bed. The only time I remembered was when I made it all the way down the stairs and outside. The softness of the grass on my cheek. I didn't remember them dragging me back upstairs. Time became a funny thing when confined to my bed. Time ebbed and flowed. Above all else, it was long. My life was on pause, frozen, the world had shrunk down to the size of my bed.

The darkness came less and less until almost gone. I did not fear the black hole, but other fears emerged and unfolded in front of me, pointed me in a direction I had no desire to travel. I remembered my sister talking to me. It could have been a dream, could have been another voice, a new voice, one that was fooling me with its talk of love, support, understanding. This could have been a new voice that turned in on itself, turned its back on me, laughing in my face, leaving me paralyzed, shaken up, pushed down. Deep in my heart, I knew it was my sister, I knew she meant what she said. Her words had slowly been pulling me back out of the darkness, so I had to believe in them.

For the first time, I had some kind of faith, a new belief, one that was applied to me. A faith that focused on me, one that helped me get better if I could get better, if I could see myself through this.

One day I faced the window. The leaves were different colours, swayed in the wind. A person walked a dog past the hospital. Stared out the window for a long time. I didn't know what a long time was anymore. The concept of time was lost on me for the moment. I didn't mind, although it scared me a bit, made me wonder if I would ever grasp the concept again or would I continue to float between seconds, minutes, hours in the dark spaces where time does not exist.

After this long time, I stepped on to my own two feet. Wobbly at first, my feet were weak. I pulled up the gown, looked at my skinny legs. I saw no muscles, took the rest of the gown off. Looked at my chest, stomach, arms - all skinny. Slowly I walked across the room into the bathroom, flipped on the light, looked in the mirror.

Shocked.

The person I saw in the mirror was not me. The only thing I recognized was the scar on my face. I turned the light off so I could not see well, so I couldn't see my hollow face. A beard covered the gauntness in my cheeks. Under the facial hair, my eyes had sunken into my skull. My eyes were thick with black circles. My hair was long, knotted. Lips chapped, mouth dry.

I left the washroom, couldn't look anymore. That was another person. I had jumped into another person's body. This was not me. Crawling back into bed, I curled up, but instantly thought, No! Jumped back out of bed, got a head rush, I could no longer lay down, it was breaking down my body, breaking down my mind. I had no resistance, no confidence, no idea of who I was, where I was, what happened.

There was a rustling of sheets from across the room. I was not alone. There was someone here, someone had followed me, had been listening. There was a sheet splitting the room in half. From the other side of the sheet, a voice, a gravelly voice said, "What's with the fucking noise, man? Keep it down would you, you've been quiet until now. Give us a break, will you?" There was more rustling of sheets. I stood still so nobody heard me, they would go away. Someone had been here, had been listening. They were here for me, wanted to do something to me. The voice spoke again, "Listen, sorry to say 'fucking' noise. I don't mean to scare you. I just need my sleep. You can move about. I'm up now, why don't we meet face-to-face? You've been here almost a month, and not a damn peep until now."

I did not move. I made a decision, took a step closer to the sheet. I was quiet, ready for anything. Stepping closer, stopped, listened for any movement. One more step. At the sheet, I put one hand on the end, took a breath, sucked air into my lungs, expanded my insides, let it all go. When I let it all go, I yanked the sheet open, and it ripped right off the rollers. A man was laying on a bed directly opposite me. He pulled the bed sheet up over his face as I jumped into his side of the room and froze like a statue. I did not move, my muscles shook with too much effort. The man slowly brought the sheet down under his chin. He was a man with the biggest cranium I had ever seen. Shaved bald. Older, maybe mid-fifties, his eyes narrowed at me, he said, "Jesus, there are easier ways to kill a man. There are easier ways to enter a room. I got a weak heart."

Quietly, I took in the man, looked at the photographs on his side table, at his chair, the books on his small shelf. "Can you talk, man?" He asked. Wetting my lips with my tongue, I asked, "Who are you?" The man dropped the sheet further down his chest, he let out a breath, a sigh, "I'm the fucking Easter Bunny, man. My name's Jim, Jimmy for short, if you like that." I said, "Jimmy is longer than Jim." He rolled his eyes, said, "Got a goddamn comedian for a roommate, do I?"

Falling silent, we had a staring contest, saw if what we said, we meant. This went on for a long time until the corners of Jimmy's mouth moved into a smile. I said, "I win, you're smiling." He said, "I ain't smiling.

Win what?" I said, "We had a stare down. You smiled, I win." He said, "What did you win?" I said, "I don't know." He said, "You are one crazy mother fucker, no wonder you're in this place. Out of all the crazy mother fuckers in here, I'm put with you." I said, "I could say the same thing." To this, he laughed, I laughed. He asked, "What've you been doing over there all this time?" I said, "Nothing." He asked no further questions. He told me to sit down on his chair. It was nice talking to a real person, someone that was there, that I thought was there, someone that was like me.

Helen walked in, smiled, said she was happy to see me up. If I were not too tired, the doctor would like to talk to me. I did not want to see him, but I would go with Helen, would go anywhere with Helen.

There was no one around, I was a little dizzy from all the activity. My first experience of the space-time continuum breaking apart happened. This was the only way I could describe it, the only way was to put it into a box, make sense of it, determine that it was not a break from reality, the way I was used to, the scary way, the way where I lost control. I convinced myself this was how I was getting better, that it was a sign, a sign that I was trying to learn something about myself, I was trying to understand something new about myself. The empty hallway became charged with electrical currents. I was hyper-aware of my insides, of the voice, although it said nothing. I could feel every particle of dust, the emptiness filled me up, spoke to me, it said something. I couldn't understand it yet. I learned one thing, learned of my desire to get better, determined that I wanted to get out of here. My life had been spent in empty dark corridors of a type of purgatory, where I was me, but a me that was someone else. I sniffed the air, the air was stale. Urine mixed in with something I only identified as food. I farted, the smell got added to the staleness. I felt the events that happened in this space. A residue of past lives. The voices murmured, they were being stirred alive, they had something to say to me, I was not ready to listen.

The door to the office opened, sounded like thunder, snapped me out of wherever I was. Helen asked me to come inside. I remembered it from when they first brought me here. Seemed like so long ago. It was long ago. The doctor sat behind his desk, smiled at me, told me he was happy that I was up, told me to take it easy for a bit. Still wasn't sure if I was awake, asleep, if this was real, if Jimmy was real, if Helen was real. I felt the chair under my ass, wondered if it was real. I nodded my head at what he said, heard nothing, just watched his mouth move, watched him scratch his pen as he made notes. What was he writing? What was he saying? I couldn't concentrate, there was something about medication, something about therapy, something about facing my issues, something about accepting who I was.

The office door burst open. A tall and skinny man stepped into the office. The air in the office instantly changed, tension filled the room, the man closed the door behind him. He brought in with him air, molecules that bounced off the walls, created alarm bells in my head that filled me up with anxiety. The man shifted from one foot to another, not manically, but small movements, methodical, rhythmic. He had long stringy hair that should be white but was more yellow, beady eyes that had seen better days. His skin was leathery, his fingers yellow and shades of brown from too many cigarettes. He needed a shave. When he opened his mouth, there was a lack of teeth to chomp food. The doctor lifted his arm with his palm facing towards the man, asked him silently to stop, the man looked at me, looked down, embarrassed. He said, "I need to speak with you, doctor. I need to talk with you right now." He looked at the doctor with pleading eyes, desperate eyes. The doctor said, "Okay Henry, okay, we will talk. I need five minutes to finish up with a patient here."

The man shifted from one foot to the other, the air in the office so thick I couldn't breath. Henry mumbled something to us, maybe to himself, maybe to someone else, he said, "Okay, I just need... I need to talk with you. You see, he's back, the man in the trench coat, he's back and he's following me." The doctor nodded his head, said, "Okay Henry, okay. I'll be five minutes and then we can talk. Can you wait five minutes?" Henry shifted, shook his head really fast. He slowed his head down until he stopped, said, "Yeah, yeah. I can wait. You just have to understand... you have to see that, well, the ghost is back. The ghost in the trench coat is back. I think someone is trying to kill me again. Someone is trying to kill me again. It's the ghost, he's back. I don't want to die." The doctor nodded his head, said, "We'll have a cigarette, how about that? Why don't you wait for me outside? I'll be right there. We'll talk about the ghost." Henry kept dancing between his feet. He mumbled to himself, nodded to himself, "Okay, I'll wait outside and we'll smoke. He doesn't know I'm here." Henry looked at me, I saw something in his eyes, I asked him, "Henry, who is the ghost?" The doctor politely asked me to refrain from speaking to Henry. I asked again, "Henry, who is the ghost?" There was no answer from Henry. He avoided my stare, mumbled, grabbed the doorknob and he was out the door.

The thickness in the air was taken with him. The doctor told me it wouldn't be such a good idea to talk to Henry. That I had my own problems and should focus on myself. I told him I was focusing on my own problems, I was just wondering what old Henry there was seeing. The doctor smiled, said, "We are done for today."

Helen guided me back to my room, she was always smiling. We reached my room, Jimmy was sleeping. Helen left, I looked out the window. Henry was pacing back and forth under a tree, smoking, mumbling to himself. My gaze shifted to my open door. Walked over, had a look out the hallway, no one around. I headed over to the stairwell, walked down the stairs, walked towards the front door. The security guard was talking to a nurse, I slipped by them.

Outside, I took in huge gulps of fresh air. Spotted Henry by the tree, approached him, called his name, he didn't hear me. Called his name again, he stopped, looked at me. His eyes narrowed, I told him we just met inside the doctor's office. He didn't recognize me. I smiled at him, it did not work. "Tell me about the ghost. What is the ghost?" He shifted around, smoked. I said, "Really, I want to know. I have my own ghost, he speaks to me over my left shoulder. He never leaves me alone." Henry stopped shifting. He looked around, said, "Where's the doctor? Why're you here? Why do you want to know about the ghost?" I said, "I don't know, maybe our ghosts are similar? Maybe they have something in common?" Henry said, "The ghost is someone that dresses in a trench coat. He dresses like everyone else but he doesn't fool me. I know him. He never says anything to me. He just watches and waits." Nodding my head, I said, "What are they waiting for Henry?" He said, "They're waiting to kill me. What does your ghost tell you?" I looked down, said, "He tells me I am less than human. He tells me I am a failure, worthless. Tells me of all the ways I can hurt myself. Tells me how to do it." Henry started pacing again, said, "Yeah, that's you, right? That's just you telling you that stuff. Can't you stop it?" I laughed, "No, Henry I cannot. Maybe it is me talking. I just don't know why I'd want to hurt myself. Why would I tell me to hurt myself?" Henry said, "Sometimes I wish he'd kill me." I shook my head, said, "Henry, you are a person. You deserve better from yourself. You don't deserve to die like that, just as I don't deserve to die. Not yet anyway, not until we are sound of mind and ready to properly make that decision." Henry started laughing, cackled, sounded like the voice, like it spoke through him. He said, "It's good that you think you have a choice in the matter, but you don't. You think you do, but you don't. Stop kidding yourself, the ghost is after you just like it's after me. There is no way out, it's just a matter of time."

An orderly grabbed me by the arm. The doctor was behind him, told me I should not be out here, should not be talking to Henry. I tried to speak, Henry cackled, drowned out my voice. I was dragged back inside, pulled upstairs, put to bed. The commotion woke Jimmy, he started yelling fucking this, fucking that. The orderly stood in our doorway, out the window the doctor sat on the ground under the tree while Henry paced around him smoking, talking, telling him about the ghost. Henry stopped pacing at one point, looked up at my window, looked right into my eyes. He saw what I was thinking, he knew what I was thinking. Knew that there was glass between me and the world, there always had been. I wanted to know how to push the glass aside, to experience things as they were, to have no barrier between me and the world. It had been here so long without me knowing it, without a way out. I had to break the glass, shatter the glass, stop me from being trapped in my own prison. I needed to feel something, to know people around me as they were, to know that I was not a failure. I was not someone else, I was me.

Voices over my left shoulder, sure, but this was not who I was, I was something more. A fire burned in me. The fire had been out, someone forgot to light it. The smoke rings curled around my insides. How do I relight my own flame? My life force that has gone out, left me hollow, an invisible man feeling like there were no options, continually knowing it was all up to me, unable to do it, to strike a match, light the flame. To see who I was, why was I afraid to see this, to know this? I broke the stare with Henry, he won this round. I let him win. I lay down on my bed, went to sleep, dreamt nothing, felt nothing, in many ways, I was nothing, but I wanted to be more.

The first therapy session revolved around the rules of the hospital I had broken – almost all of them already. They asked me how I felt, I told them numb. Told them I did not know who I was. I wished I could have said more, wished I could have told them all that I knew. The fact was, I did not see the truth, it eluded me.

Back to my room, slept more, ate, went to more therapy sessions. The hospital became routine. In the mirror, I looked at myself every morning to catch a glimpse of the person I was, to see if there was a person there. Disappointed every morning, I continued on. Every day became the same. Felt no better, no worse. Medicated. Talked with Jimmy every afternoon. I sat on a chair, he lay on his bed. We did not talk about why we were here, we talked about other things. The hospital, gossiped about Helen, wondered about her life, who she was, why she worked here. Jimmy was my friend.

There were nightly conversations with the voice. It spoke over my left shoulder, asked me why I was here, I told it to stop. The voice laughed, told me I would never get rid of it, was stuck with it. The voice called me names, told me this was not helping, it would not help, I would forever hear voices, I would always be inside a box, be outside of normal. The voice laughed at me, cackled. I wanted it to stop, I was not able to stand up to it yet.

It was the truth when I said I felt numb but there were times when an emotion so great came over me. This emotion flowed through me. This emotion started low in my belly like a laugh, but it was not a laugh. It flew up my spine, hit me right between the eyes, turned a faucet on and I cried, wept silently in my bed at night. Wept for myself, for my poor sister that deserved more, for my parents, my dead mother, my deadbeat father. I wept, thankful that it happened only at night, so no one knew it happened. So loud some nights I was afraid Jimmy would waken. He never said anything. Wept for the shell that had become my body, the mind that was too weak to decipher reality from fantasy, for my heart that ached to be understood. The voice spoke to me, offered its help, wondered why I no longer answered its questions, why I ignored it.

Above all else, I experienced loneliness like never before. Something in me had died. This was a good thing, perhaps it was the illness that was dying, maybe the delusions that had taken over my mind for most of my life were finally going to leave me in peace. This was what I wanted - peace. I wanted to be left alone.

For that first year at the hospital, I wanted to be forgotten. I could barely last a few hours before having to lay down again, to feel the mattress under my body, to escape into a world of nothingness. Regressed to the point where I found no hope, no hope in the days that were laid out in front of me. They seemed endless, presenting before me a life that was not worth living.

The voice had often talked to me of suicide. The voice wanted me to do it, but in the end, something did snap in my head to show me that I should not go through with it. Now as I was meeting myself, the true self behind the different masks I had been wearing for so long, I found nothing, only numbness. Saw someone I did not like because there was no substance, nothing to grasp on to, just an empty vessel that said nothing, did not respond to anything, had no desire to live another day.

Thoughts of suicide pervaded my mind in those early days. I took them very seriously, I knew that this was the real me talking, it was not the voice persuading me to do something. It was slowly becoming my choice, it was me that was talking, my voice telling me that there was nothing to live for. I started looking for ways to end it in, every corner of the hospital, during every meal, every therapy session.

I often stared out of the window. I was heavily medicated, and it took a toll on me physically, pushed my will around, made it into something weak, something I could not rely on. Staring out the window, my eyes became small slits. Stared at the tree, the leaves, looking for Henry, wondering if I would see him again. I wanted to know more about the ghost, wanted to see if it was the same ghost as mine. Never saw him again, never saw anyone under that tree. The leaves turned green, turned brown, fell off, snow came, snow went. The tree stood unmoving, growing steadily, changing into something new, while I stayed the same with the same routine every day. Eat, shit, sleep, talk, therapy, blah blah blah.

I became disgusted with my life, unable to move, make decisions. Finally, there was a free choice, I was not being guided by anything over my left shoulder. The voice spoke to me less and less. I felt an emptiness without it, felt I had once again been abandoned and even something like that had given up on me. Hated the fact that I was so selfish, moping around, feeling unmoved by the daily wonders of life. All was lost on me, I had to do something. Some days I mustered my strength, summoned thoughts that told me I was going to change things, this day was going to be different. I saw a new day, a new way, but the strength left as quickly as it arrived. I would soon be back laying on my bed, staring out the window, wondering who I was, what I should do, what I was doing here.

Apparently, this was progress, this was normal. The emptiness was a sign I was rebuilding myself. Nodded my head, hung my head, listened to what I was told. I felt forgotten like any number of people that walked through these halls. A nobody, a number, a person in a bed that got better or would not get better, would kill himself or not kill himself.

The loneliness followed me around the hallways.

When I stopped, turned around, looked, nothing. Just hung my head slightly, shook my head, I didn't care either way, the fire inside was drowning. It was difficult to describe what I felt when I lay there on that bed. My eyes could not focus on anything. My eyes watered, which made me blink every so often. My thoughts bounced from one thing to another like a pinball machine, only there were no points in this game. Things passed along in front of my eyes or in front of my mind. I saw them, just did not care, felt nothing either way.

Deep inside that well, getting deeper every day, falling, digging my own way down. Maybe I thought I could keep digging and reach somewhere? Dig so far that I would dig a hole out the other side of the earth, be in a different country, become a different person? Or maybe I was digging to just dig to get farther down to return to the darkness?

It was a long year, a year that I thought I was dying a slow death, a slow suicide. One that was perpetrated by me, initiated by choice. The contents of my mind were thrown away, left with nothing. I would soon have to face the choice of rebuilding this or throwing the body out with the mind. Not yet ready to make that choice, so I lay in my bed, ate, therapy, watched the tree outside my window. The loneliness curled up on the bed with me, it was my only true friend beside Jimmy, the only friend I felt I could rely on.

After a year in the hospital, not much had changed. I ventured in and out of the darkness, sometimes it engulfed me entirely for days, sometimes I was downright cheery with Jimmy and with Helen and even with the doctor. I really did not know why I was there. I heard voices, so what? Didn't everyone hear voices? Every morning I woke up, looked in the mirror - my cheeks were filling in. Shaved every day, kept myself clean, figured that was something, a step in the right direction.

In my sessions with the doctor, he asked me what the voices said. I told him, figured I had nothing to lose. My life consisted of three rooms: my bedroom, the lunchroom, and the doctor's office. I shuffled from one room to another, not caring, not seeing me for what I was, not finding anything, not moving forward, just passing the time.

The voice spoke to me often over my left shoulder. The voice told me many things. It talked mostly about me, what I should be doing, what I should be saying to the doctor, to Helen. I never did what it told me to do. On good days, I ignored it. On bad days, I did not get out of bed.

Back in the doctor's office, we had not spoken for almost fifteen minutes. We sat staring at each other until he finally said, "I see you are in one of your silent moods." He shifted around in his chair. I nodded. He said, "You have been here for one year. I have a question for you." He paused here. I did not know if he wanted me to say something. He continued, "Do you want to get better?" We sat there for another fifteen minutes. I stared at him, didn't blink. He waited for an answer. I waited for an answer, until I finally said,

"I don't feel sick. I don't think I am sick. How can a person get better if he doesn't know that he is ill?" It was now the doctor's turn to be silent. When he was deep in thought, he chewed on his pencil. A large cup of chewed up pencils sat on his desk. He should be careful of lead poisoning. Finally took the pencil out of his mouth, said, "That's a good question. So, you do not think you're ill?" I answered quickly, I didn't like all this silence anymore, "No, I do not think I am ill. I don't feel good. I feel far from good. I have always felt this way. I sit here in front of you and I have told you all about my life. I have said all I am going to say for now because there is nothing more to say. I have always felt like this. I have no frame of reference, it has become my life, the structure, the backbone which I have never gotten used to. Up, down, sideways, the days I cannot get out of bed. It is painful but what else am I to do? How do I get better if I do not know what better is? If these symptoms that I know so well are symptoms of some illness or some disease, what is it? Tell me! I will work to get better. I just don't know what it is. I am numb to everything you have told me. The past year feels like an eternity. I feel no better, no worse, just the same as always. I am not seeing things, believing in things as easily as before, but how do I know this is not a delusion in itself? How do I know I am not in some other stage of this illness?"

The doctor was quiet. I was standing. I did not realize it. I continued, "Tell me! What is the cure? What is it? How do I stop from thinking these thoughts? What are these thoughts? What is wrong? What is right? Where do I go from here? What is it you want me to do? I would surely like to know! Would I like to get better? Yes! What kind of a condescending question is that to ask a patient? One of your best patients, a patient that has been here for a year, struggling, laying in his bed for days on end, engulfed in darkness, voices echoing in my ears, whispering over my shoulders. Unable to move, some days unable to gather the strength or the energy to move, experiencing dreams so painful that I wrestle with myself through the night, scratch at my neck, wake with red marks on my throat, cracked fingernails. If I am broken, fix me, tell me how to fix me. I'll do it, I will fix it. I know I can. I know I can learn to feel the difference between being ill and being normal. Just tell me what it is." I had been pacing around the room. My voice was loud. The doctor said, "Thank you for telling me all of that. This is the problem: you have improved more in the last ten minutes than in the last year. You look exhausted because you spoke to me through your emotions, you spoke from your heart. Up until now, you have been telling me facts. You might as well have taken out a laundry list of what has happened in your life, but you have not told me what is behind those facts. What is driving the creation of those facts? Why have you had these experiences your entire life? Why you cannot tell the difference between them? That is what we are after, that is what will help you."

Silence.

I just didn't know what to say. A wire had been cut

that ran from my heart to my mind. I wanted it fixed, to exist here in this world. I looked at the doctor. I had tears in my eyes. I tried not to cry in front of him, he saw my tears anyways. He nodded at me, smiled, said, "That's enough today. We've talked long enough. I want to hear more of this. I want to hear more of what is behind the facts. You want to know how you can get better? It is not looking to me, looking to others around you. It is the ability to look inside, see what is there, feel what is there, try to make adjustments inside of yourself. Determine for yourself what is right. Find that voice that is your voice and listen to that voice. The other ones might be here with you for a long time, they might be here with you forever. It is up to you to make decisions about the direction you are going towards. It is your choice." I said to him, "That is easy to say." He grunted, even laughed. It was the first time I had seen him laugh and it made me laugh. I tried not to laugh, wiped away the tears. I did not let them run down my cheeks, not today, not then.

Leaving his office, I thought about choice. About decisions. About my insides, and how they had never cooperated with me, why would they start now? Why would they listen to me now? I walked down the hallway, they trusted me to be by myself sometimes. I stopped at the window, looked out, saw the tree. It started raining, the thick raindrops thumped against the glass. I saw a hundred tiny reflections of myself in the raindrops - which one was the real me?

I wished I could say it was something more dramatic

than a kiwi, but there it was: a kiwi every day. Shuffled down to lunch, sat by myself. Sometimes, if in the mood, I sat beside Jimmy, but not today. Waited in line, grabbed a tray, the tray heavy in my hands, it got heavier as food piled on. The last thing I got was a kiwi. On this day, the day I spoke with the doctor, where I wondered who I was, wondered if I wanted to get better, wondered what getting better meant. I sat down before my tray of food, I was not hungry, as usual. I stared at that kiwi, felt like the kiwi stared back at me. It was a kiwi, large, with a furry exterior. The kiwi transmitted information to me, telling me something or trying to tell me something. I stared at that kiwi, used my imagination, imagined it was the last kiwi on earth, it was the last piece of food. This was it, there was nothing left after this kiwi, it would not be long until I perished. Dreamt of that kiwi, the way it tasted, my mouth watered at the thought, my parched throat would be swelled, swallowed imagined pieces of kiwi. My ears remembered the softness when I bit into it.

Everything went away from me at that moment, the voice over my shoulder said nothing. I wondered if the voice finally decided I was not worth it anymore. I picked up the kiwi, felt the weight in my hand. It would be the last time I ever lifted a kiwi, the last time I felt its heaviness. I turned it around in my hand, explored it, investigated it, put to memory every small dent and imperfection. Lifted it to my face, looked through it. Moved it to my mouth, parted my lips, sunk my teeth into the skin, breaking it, feeling the juices flow into my mouth.

It was glorious.

The last kiwi in the world.

The last piece of food in the world.

It was mine, all mine.

Sliced a piece with my teeth, dropped it into my mouth, let it lay there, sloshed it around inside, sucked on it, finally breaking it up into small pieces, swallowing the pieces. It was without a doubt the most delicious, most satisfying mouthful that I had ever experienced. The small pieces moved down my throat, through my chest, moved around my insides, slipped into my stomach. My entire body thanked me as the kiwi pieces dissolved. I took another bite and another bite, savouring each piece, chomping it into small pieces, sucking the juices, knowing that with each bite I was getting closer to the end. I didn't care. I took each piece as it came, treated each of them equally. My lips, the area around my mouth was wet with juice. I used my tongue, licked it, not wanting to waste anything. Sucked on my fingers, sucked the juice that dripped off the peels. Bite after bite, I did not rush, did not speed up. I ate methodically, ate so I could think about what I was eating. No voice spoke to me. I expected it to tell me how ridiculous this was, but I did not care. I was eating my last meal, this was it, the only thing to look forward to was death from starvation after this lonely kiwi. I made my way around the kiwi, tackled the top, the bottom. Stared at the last piece, knew that I was dying after this. I ate that last piece, felt it all mix together in my stomach.

I just accomplished something I had rarely felt - enjoyment. I sat to relish in this enjoyment. I had eaten my last kiwi, my last morsel of food. I knew this was the start of something. I did not know what, I did not think about it. I sat there with a kiwi in my stomach.

The light from the windows seemed to change, the sun snuck out from under some dirty clouds, its rays penetrated the glass, showed shadows from trees, from tables, chairs, other patients. The rays moved quickly, sprayed across the tables, reached my face, reflected off my eyes. Tears ran down my cheeks. I let them, I did not move. I did not cry because I was sad, I cried because of joy. I cried as a release.

I appreciated the kiwi, thanked it for giving itself to me, cried because my insides seemed to become illuminated. My insides wanted to bust out of me, bloat my body so I grew weightless, passed through the walls, through the ceiling, moved up into the sky, floating through the air. They knew it was my last kiwi, my last bite of food. My insides, including my mind, were okay with this. We were all okay.

Cleaned off my tray, thanked the person slopping out the food, returned to my room. I said, "Hello!" Jimmy squinted at me in my good mood. I lay down on my bed, stood up. Did not want to sleep, did not want to lay down. Walked the hallways, saw Helen, waved to her, said, "Hello!" It was time for group therapy, I sat in the room with five others. Usually, I said not a word, that day they could not shut me up, that day I had suggestions for others, had insights into myself. They scowled at me, but as I kept talking, kept saying things, kept looking at people in the eyes, spoke from my heart, connected my heart to my mind, sent messages from my heart to my mind. I was able to communicate what I wanted with words. They clapped for me at the end, the doctor turned to me, thanked me for my contributions, smiled. Everyone clapped, patted me on the back. I was a bit confused about this, shrugged my shoulders, thought of my kiwi. I still tasted the kiwi.

The next morning, I felt better than I had in a long time. Went through my morning with hardly a thought.

Lunchtime.

I went through the lineup, ignored the smells of the food, my mouth dropped when I saw my kiwi. I grabbed it, sat down, stared at it. Rejoiced that I was able to have another one, that I was lucky enough that yesterday was not my last one. Undoubtedly this was the last one. I convinced myself there were no more after this. Somehow it was better than the one yesterday, was fuller, juicier. I tasted every drop of it, felt it fall through my body. I thanked the kiwi.

I knew this was the last one.

I appreciated every bite. Drank it up. After I was done, I looked around, looked in the faces of the other patients, wondering if they felt the same thing as I did, wondered if they felt so lucky to have their kiwi. It seemed so small, thinking of a kiwi in these terms. It was, after all, only a kiwi. Almost everyone had access to these green jewels. I was starting from zero, starting from nothing, I needed something to hold on to. Needed a reference from which to measure. The kiwi made me feel better. It made me feel appreciated as a human being, that I needed this kiwi to survive, and it needed me. We worked together to breathe life back into these bones, to shape something, to recreate a human being, to try to understand what that meant, what it meant to once again be a person that was making his own decisions. To not only want to get better but understand genuinely from the inside what it meant to get better, to not walk but run towards it. Open the door without knocking.

I went to bed every night knowing I had eaten my last kiwi. I woke every morning wondering, hoping there might be a kiwi waiting for me in the lunch room. I surprised myself with wonder at the sight of the kiwi. Cut into it, felt it go down, nourishing my insides. I learned how to be human again, learning from a fundamental level that I was a person, someone who had thoughts in his head. An individual that was maybe different, maybe someone that heard things in his head, heard other people talking. I just started ignoring them, filled my thoughts with the kiwi. My senses exploded with the taste, with the smell of the kiwi.

After weeks of eating the kiwis slowly during my lunchtime, I started noticing other things. The tree outside my window, knowing that it gave life, that its leaves fell in the winter time, that they grew back because it was alive and I was alive. I looked at the tree with the same appreciation as the kiwi.

I walked down the hallway, saw Helen, drank in her smile with my eyes, stopped her, talked to her only to hear the sound of her voice, to give a present to my ears. The sunlight crawled across the lunchroom floor. The sun provided the tree life, the tree helped give us life. I sat in the sunshine, drew strength from it, felt its rays bouncing off my skin, entering inside.

I went through all my routines with new found energy. Talking out of turn, passing people in the hallway and not caring what they thought of me, just wondering what was going on in their head, hoping they could gain access to the same thoughts that I had. I sat beside Jimmy, read to him. He never asked me, I just picked up a book from his shelf one day, sat on his chair, started reading. He had a confused look on his face, I didn't care. After a few days of this, he expected it. I read the words as though I discovered how to read for the first time. I was determining language, communication, the ability for words on a page to speak to people, to have a voice of their own, a different voice, one that spoke a language we all could feel inside, one that was different for each of us, but one we felt in our hearts.

I accumulated a list of items, seeing things for what they were. Eating my kiwi every day, every day it was my last kiwi. I felt the sun when it set, imagined I would never see it again, only to wake with it sprayed across my face, and I said, "Hello!" to the sun hitting my face. At first, I could not put my finger on what was stirring me up inside. I wondered if this was what feeling better meant? I soon discovered it was something I had never felt before, it was something new to me, it was called hope. When the word popped into my head, it spread across my lips. I played with the word, said it over and over. I knew what it was, knew what it meant for the first time in my life. I knew what it must have felt like. Hope arrived at my table, got me out of bed. Hope that came in the shape of a kiwi.

Chapter Four

The kiwi was revelatory to me. In the hospital, I entered afraid and scared of myself, my surroundings, others. The voice was there, always there. I worked at different forms of acceptance, of trying to understand what it was that ailed me. Why this voice spoke to me, why it chose me.

After months of patience, months of eating a kiwi every day, of forcing myself to believe every day was my last one, a belief in other things emerged. Small details appeared in my field of vision in ways that were not possible before. From the kiwi perspective, the tree outside my window gave me life, gave life to everyone around it. The tree radiated a life force in subtle, unspoken ways. How many times had I sat under a tree, thanked it for its natural process of providing me with oxygen? Thanked it for providing shade from a hot sun? Shelter from the rain?

The doctor and nurses rewarded my progress, granted me more freedom. I was allowed to walk outside in the forest of trees behind the hospital. The hospital was located away from the city, far from the tar of bad air, cars, noise. I walked all day in the forest, wandered, lost in my thoughts, never saw the same tree twice. At first, I was under supervision, which was okay because usually, Helen accompanied me for my walk. She liked it, the walks got her out of the hospital.

There were so many people in Helen's care in different mindsets. All the people, the severe cases the doctor had to work hard at to bring back from the darkness. I struggled so long, lived in my shadow, never aware that someone had it worse than me. Within the walls of the hospital, many were forgotten, never to return. I thought I was a lost cause. I felt guilty about this, but it gave me the confidence to know that I could get better, had the strength to get better. Others were not so lucky.

A walk with Helen every day, even if it rained. Besides the kiwi perspective, the walks saved me. We were usually alone in the woods. The path crude. As we walked, we talked. She helped me develop what she called small talk: a form of conversation that had little meaning but which I engaged people in to get to know them better and segue into discussions with more depth.

The palm of my hand touched every tree. Sometimes I felt a pulse running from the tree into my hand like electricity. Imagined the trees had hearts. They were connected to their function, had personalities. Some had branches that slumped, these were the insecure trees. Some had branches that stood straight up, these were the confident trees, they knew exactly what was going on.

After a while the doctor allowed me to walk on my own. This was my favourite part of the day. In keeping with the kiwi perspective, I first imagined that the kiwi was my last one. I enjoyed it, felt it rumble around in my stomach. With my running shoes on, getting ready for my walk, I believed it would be my final one. The last time I saw the trees, the last time I felt their pulse gather strength from their roots. On my way into the woods, I said to them in my head, *Hi, aren't you happy to see me?* On my way out of the woods, I said, *Goodbye, thank you!* No sadness after my kiwi, no sorrow after my walks. I knew I got the most from them, knew that I was stronger, felt something stranger than hope, stranger than strength, I felt happy.

My sister came to see me. I convinced myself I would never see her again, but she walked into my room and the light changed. We ate in the lunchroom, I gave her half of my kiwi. I knew it would be my last kiwi forever. I wanted to make sure my sister got half of it. We went out for a walk through the trees, I told her all about them. We walked all day, I talked and talked, she barely got a word in. She stopped me while we walked in the woods, lightly grabbed me by the arm, turned me to face her, looked into my eyes, made sure I was listening, she said, "I wanted you to know that I'm proud of you. I wanted to tell you that you are becoming an adult, someone I always have been happy to call my brother. Now, through all that you have become, I am so happy that you are coming out of this, that you are getting better." My sister started tearing up, but she controlled it, I said back to her, "I am proud of you too. I would not be standing here without you." She looked down, I continued on, "No really. Who else was there for me? No one. We only have each other. I think we have done a good job at holding it together despite everything." She put her arm around me, we continued walking, siblings alone in this world, unable to rely on anyone else. We would have crumbled on our own, lost it a long time ago. We kept each other's fire going, made sure it never went out. We would always be there for each other.

We walked all day, sat next to each other on a rock, watched the sun go down. She promised me she would visit more. I knew she could not, I wished she could, but she had business commitments. I was content for now to be here on my own, to sort through my mind. Out by her car, she gave me a hug. We stood still with our arms around each other, did not move until I could not breathe. She laughed, said, "I didn't want to let go. I'll be back soon." The car went into the distance until it was gone. I was not sad, I imagined that was the last time I would see her. I evaluated our visitation, I was happy with it, went to sleep clear headed.

This was a process of cleaning out my head, getting rid of the stuff I no longer wanted, that no longer needed to be there. When I started this process, I did not realize just how much was up there. Overpopulated. Lots of shovelling, removing what I couldn't use. The voice yelled at me every day, told me it would all come back. Threatened me, called me names. I had bad days but somehow continued moving, continued shovelling. My mind used to race, buzzed constantly. Thoughts entered, jumped around, left without me even knowing they were there, but some thoughts left a residue imprinted on my brain I needed to get rid of. Some of these imprinted thoughts quietly went if I asked them. Others I needed to extract. They screamed, shouted, did not want to leave. Thoughts jumped into my mind at all times. While eating my kiwi or when falling asleep, usually a feeling of high anxiety rose in me, took over my body until I could not function, paralyzing me.

A few weeks ago, I discovered I had a box inside me like a jack in the box. It was opened long ago, allowing unspeakable thoughts to run around my insides. I constructed another box, one to pack everything back into, to send it away from me with a one-way ticket someplace else. By pushing these feelings away, it created other feelings throughout my insides. So I had to deal with these. I built another box for feelings that I did not really want to get rid of. I might need them on another day but were causing trouble at the moment.

Everything rose to my head through a complicated

wiring system. Anxieties filled my brain up, I pushed them back down. I imagined feelings were a physical entity that I could stuff into one of my boxes. The In Box and the Out Box. The Out Box got taken out with the trash every week, represented feelings and thoughts that I did not need anymore. The In Box were feelings that caused me trouble but which I might need later. All kinds of things started coming up to my brain, and I got lots of practice in pushing them back down. I became stronger every time I sent something south. Every box I left out in the trash, the thoughts came up sometimes about what someone said about me. Could be a memory of something I did not even remember happening to me. If I wanted to keep it, into the In Box, if not, out with the Out Box.

All kinds of new discoveries! I was happy about certain things. Kept every memory, every thought I had about my sister. She stayed with me at all times. Everything the voice said went into the Out Box. There were many things - that box was overflowing on some days. I was emptying myself out. I tried not to think, but since this was hard to do, I tried to think only good thoughts. Grabbed on to those good thoughts with both hands, did not want to ever let go of them.

There were certain things I wanted to know about with my condition. I started to read a lot. I asked the doctor for books about my condition. He obliged, provided me with book after book. Devoured the books, kept most of those thoughts. I investigated myself, discovered new methods in which I could empty out my mind. I learned about the medications I was taking, what was in each pill. I asked Jimmy what his symptoms were, guessed his diagnosis, which was cheating because I already knew what was wrong with him. I walked around the hospital, interviewed other patients. Some thought I was a doctor. I made notes, compared them with my books. I wrote up fake papers that outlined their symptoms, what might have caused them, what medications they should be on, what else they could be doing to help make themselves better. Of course, these notes were all just for my eyes.

I met all kinds of people, did a lot of small talk. Some even went further with me, they actually seemed to like talking with me. The voice was jealous, filled in what it believed they really thought. I just did not like what it had to say anymore. I wanted to talk to real people in front of me that were living, breathing, sad, happy, that were interested in what I had to say, not just interested in criticizing me, filling my head up with Out Box thoughts.

I stared at the ceiling. Not a blank stare with nothing in my head except the sound of the voice commenting on everything. This was a new stare, one where new thoughts danced across my mind, just inside my forehead. These were thoughts I wanted to keep, wanted to hold on to. Inquisitive thoughts, wondering what happened outside these walls, thinking about what happened in the cities of the world, wanting to see things I have never seen before instead of feelings of fear, of emptiness.

Walked, touched every tree I came upon. Walked for a long time, longer than ever before. I knew this because I came to a small lake. It was here all along, maybe it was not here all along, perhaps it just decided to show itself, allowed me to see it? I never learned how to swim, the present moment was as good a time as ever. Stripped off my clothes, stepped into the water. Butt naked. The water cold, different than the water from the shower, the water from the facet. A new kind of energy, one more electric than even the trees. The molecules danced around my feet, bumped into my ankles, said, *Hello! Excuse Me!* The water clear, the rays of the sun sliced right through. I could see clear to the bottom, could see tiny fish swimming in parallel. At first, they sped away from me, so I stopped moving, stood very still, so still I felt my pulse in my ankles in the water. The fish came back, swam around my feet, kissed my skin. I absorbed the strength they gave me. I said in my mind, *Hello there fish! Thanks for the memories!* Could not stand here forever, took a step into the water, another step. The fish did not swim away, they stayed close, they wanted to protect me, wanted me to learn how to swim, to help me feel the freedom of floating through the water like you were flying through the air.

The water got colder.

Paused to get used to the cold. I stepped deeper into the water, the fish kissed my butt as I lowered in. Closed my eyes, dunked the rest of my body up to my head. Scared to look while under, afraid I might be blinded.

The fish kissed my cheeks, my forehead. They stuck to my ears, wondering what I was doing down here. So quiet, everything went away after lowering my head. So quiet, all I heard was the sound of my heart beating away.

No distractions, I felt the connection between my heart and my mind as they fixed each other, tying up loose ends. A series of tiny construction workers with neon vests that had X's on the front and on the back. They wore hard hats and steel-toed boots. They were doing a difficult job, one that took a long time. They had brought in small cement trucks to fill in the gaps, drills, and machines that fixed the broken connection. Not like before because I believed even when I was born, it was already broken. Replaced the connection entirely. Gave me new wires where information, communication, dialogue traveled between my heart, my mind. My heart sent a message, said, *Hello!* That was just the kind of heart it was. My mind sent a message down to my heart, it said, *How is the weather down there?* Because my mind was a joker. Messages came from everywhere, told me to surface, that I needed oxygen. Stood up out of the water, feasted on the air around me.

Spotted a tree that had branches hanging out over the water. Walked over to the tree, climbed it. How funny this would be if someone walked by? Here was this guy in the buff climbing a tree. Usually embarrassed, today I did not care, almost hoped someone walked by. How different it felt when you climbed a tree in the buff. Then realized I had never climbed a tree. Laughed, like out loud! Crawled out on the branch, the branch swayed down, up, I did not want it to break, did not want to hurt the tree. The ground looked farther away than I remembered. Remembered that I could not swim, could not see through the surface of the water, could not see how deep. Shrugged my shoulders, let out a fart. Farting was a completely different experience in the buff. Heard some creaking, the tree told me, *Jump! Come on, shit or get off the pot!*

I jumped off the branch! Well, not really jumped, more fell off. I would not compete in Olympic diving, at least not at this moment. I was not in the air long. Floated until I almost froze in the air, when all of a sudden, I crashed through the water. Cold. The shock of the fall, of the cold water, knocked the smile off my face. Knocked the wind out of my lungs. I gasped for air, water entered my mouth, sailed down my throat into my lungs. Made me gag, the gagging only made me swallow more water. I flailed my arms, my legs, there was nothing to hold on to. It was deep over here, so deep I thought about the fish, wondered if they know something I did not. The voice sprung back over my left shoulder, berated me for climbing the tree, for jumping in the water and doing all this in the buff. How embarrassing when they pulled my body out from the bottom of the lake, if they ever found my body. Pathetic, weak, could not even swim at my age.

A discovery was found deep in that lake. Something curious.

Another voice appeared, not the voice over my left

shoulder. A different one, a voice that came from my heart. The voice said, *Stop fighting it, stop flailing your arms, your legs. Just relax, allow the water to flow through you.* I obeyed it, stopped moving, felt the energy flow around me. The energy changed direction, travelled right through my body. I opened my eyes, only darkness.

Nothing.

Looked down below me, a light illuminated the way. It was dim at first but only at first. It grew strong, grew fast. I moved my arms, my feet in a controlling way. A thought popped into my head: I was swimming. It felt natural like I had been doing it all my life. I pushed down towards the light, felt like I was getting closer, but it remained the same length from me. Admired it from a distance, watched it dance through the thickness of the water. Another voice spoke, it was not my heart, this time it was my mind. It told me to go up to the surface. I obeyed this voice, changed direction, moved upwards. The surface was different from the light. Broke through the surface. The water parted across my face. I thought I would be gasping for air, I was utterly calm.

Waded over to the shore, pulled myself up on to the grass, rolled over on my back, looked at the sky. The tree that gave me entrance to the lake was silhouetted against the sky. The sun crept between the branches. Tears formed in my eyes. I did not know why. I did not think, let them fall. They fell like rain. It was the water I swallowed, it was coming out of my eyes, escaping. I knew this was not true, I knew these tears were coming from a place inside that I had not seen yet. A place I am not ready to visit.

Nothing moved in me except for the tears until the sun disappeared below the tops of the trees. I said in my mind to the sun, *Goodnight!* To the lake, *Thank you!* To the fish, *Bless you!*

Back at the hospital, Helen was worried about me. She covered for me, knew I would be back, knew how I liked my walks among the trees. Went to bed thinking about tomorrow, about what could happen. What would I see? Surely something good. I drifted off to sleep knowing I almost died. My In Box and Out Box the only reason I was alive laying in this bed. As I moved thoughts in and out of my mind and got rid of what I did not need, it made room for new experiences. Made room as my heart and my mind told me things, told me to slow down, relax, look around at the world, look and take it all in, appreciate the kiwis, the trees, the lakes, the fish. They were here for us, we were here for them. Take it all in, everything, do not look back, think about right now, think about tomorrow. Hold on to THAT, grab on to it, store it up, fill up your mind with questions then try to answer those questions. Above all else, listen to us, we are who you are, we know what is best, we feel, we think, we will guide you to new places and things you have never seen before. I went to sleep, I said to my heart, *Thank you!* I said to my mind, *We are together again.*

Every day I walked out to the lake. On my way, I

thought it would not be there, convinced myself it was all a dream, it never happened, a creation of my mind or maybe the voice wanting to lure me into a trap. The voice planning something. Every day the lake sat where it always was, and I stripped off my clothes, said to the fish, *Hello!* They kissed my ankles, the fish said, *Welcome back!* I swam back and forth across the lake. With every stroke, stronger. With every stroke, I was becoming a better swimmer. I always went to the tree that opened the entrance to the lake. Swam down deep into the water. I never saw the light again, it was gone for good, it was gone forever. I was okay with that, believed it was there for me to see one time, for me to remember and that was all. At the lake in the woods, I worked on physical strength. If my heart and my mind worked together, my body had to keep them connected, it had to be strong. I swam every day, walked every day.

The doctor allowed me to sit outside at night, a privilege few patients had. I stayed close to the hospital, was not ready to go into the woods at night. There was a bench behind the hospital from where I watched the stars. The stars filled the sky. Being so far from the city, there were no intrusive lights to block out the stars. Helen told me that the stars we saw had already burned up, already died far away. We only saw the residue years and years later. I watched the stars every night, wondered how this was possible. The stars were there but not there. I asked Helen, "Why do the same stars keep appearing if they were dead?" She did not know the answer to it.

One day after my kiwi, I walked past the recreation room. This was the space where there were couches, televisions. A place where we were supposed to socialize with each other. I usually avoided this place, glanced through the doorway as I walked by. There was a crowd around the television that peaked my curiosity. When I stepped inside, nobody noticed me. I crept closer. I did not like television, fired too much information at me, filled my mind up with many thoughts that just ended up in the Out Box. On the screen was a movie. I walked in on a scene, it seemed to take place a long time ago. There were knights, elves with pointy ears, little men. They fought these evil looking creatures. Wanting to leave, something told me to stay. I pulled up a chair. The story was an adventure story. The little people seemed to have something very important that they travelled across vast lands to destroy. They had a companion that was a creature who looked foul, I smelled him through the screen. He convinced them he was good. I knew better. What grabbed me was the landscapes the travellers moved through. An environment so beautiful, so full of trees, mountains, lakes, flatlands, more mountains. Whenever the characters went inside, whenever they were talking, I wanted them to stop talking, to start walking again. My mouth watered at the sight, at the thought. Where was this? The movie ended, left pictures in my mind, places I wanted to go, places I never knew existed. Everyone left the recreation room, I stayed seated, stared at the screen, the blank screen. With my mind, I replayed some of the scenes. I watched myself walk up mountains, swam in lakes surrounded by trees, it was glorious. Finally shook it off, went for my walk. Touched the trees, wondered about the cousins of my trees here that I saw in the movie. Where was that place? I had to find out. I swam, my thoughts were filled with pictures. Floated through the lake on my back, looked up at the sky, thought about how those mountains existed under this same sky. I saw them, I just had to find them.

The next day, it rained, which kept me indoors, but I still wanted to go for my walk. Something told me to have a look around the floors, talk to people, maybe someone knew the place I was looking for. On the third floor at the end of the hallway, there was a bench that looked out the window. On the bench was an old woman, staring out the window. I knew that look. I did something I would not usually do - sat down next to her. She did not acknowledge me at first, I was okay with that. I was going over and over in my head what I should say, having the loudest argument. My heart told me to relax, so I relaxed, opened my mouth, said, "It is beautiful isn't it?" She looked at me, she did not move, finally she nodded her head. A faint smile crossed her lips. Congratulations to me. She knew I was here. I did not know why I was talking to this lady, but I was, I said, "The trees give us strength." She turned back towards me, let out a little laugh. I did not think she was laughing at me. It was a laugh where she was laughing with me – there was a difference. If I had figured anything out, I had figured that out. She said, "Yes they do." She talked funny, had some sort of accent. The accent sounded British, but I could not be sure. It sounded like a funny British accent. I had to get her talking. I asked her, "Did you see the movie yesterday?" A smile came across her face, she nodded her head, she said, "Yes, that is my home." I tried to figure out her accent, it was not Australian. I was concentrating so hard on her accent, I did not realize at first she said it was her home. This finally registered, I calmed down, I said, "Your home?" She sighed, nodded her head. She said, "I am from New Zealand. They shot that movie all in New Zealand." I nearly farted right then and there with the luck I was having. I could not believe what she said, so I asked, "And all those places they travelled through, all those mountains, they can be found in New Zealand?" She nodded her head some more, smiled as though she remembered something far away. She said, "Yes, everything is there. My heart is there." I was so blinded by the information, I did not even notice what she might have meant by her heart. I had just one more question, I asked, "How far is New Zealand from here?" She laughed at that, she said, "It is on the other side of the world. It is far away from here." She turned towards the window, I turned towards the window with her. There was something more to what she was saying, her words had a weight that eluded me. I stood up, I said, "Thank you!" She called after me, "Don't you want to know more? Come and see me anytime. It was nice talking to someone." She turned back towards the window.

I headed off in a hurry to the recreation room. In addition to the television and the couches, there were shelves along one wall that held books, too many books really, for any of us to read. I entered the room, scanned the shelves, looked for New Zealand, looked for anything relating to this magical place. I read the spine of every book, nothing came close. Slumped down in a chair for the first time in a long time, I felt terrible. Helen saw me slumped in the chair, she came over, asked me what was wrong. I told her the whole story about the movie, about the old lady, about New Zealand. She told me she was glad I was making friends. I told her I did not even know the old lady's name. She said that was okay, just ask her next time. I told her that was not high on my list of priorities at the moment. She told me not to get snippy.

My mind was cloudy. I forgot to go outside, to look at the stars. I woke up, the kiwi tasted like a kiwi. I knew I would have another one tomorrow. Skipped my walk - that was two days in a row. I sat down in a chair in front of the television, filled my mind up with game shows, stared out the window, shovelled out the unwanted information into the Out Box. There seemed to be too much of it.

Back to my room, sitting on my bed was a book about New Zealand. The book was packed with photographs. Bowled over, I looked at the first page, drank it in. The mountains were the same as the movie, they existed. They were not fake. I turned the page, more mountains. Turned the page, water, lakes, oceans. Turned the page, flipped through the whole book, I felt Helen watching me from the doorway. When the book was finished, when there were no more pictures, I turned towards her, she was smiling, I smiled back.

I told her I was going for my walk, she nodded her head at me, she said, "Okay but there is someone that wants to visit you first." Helen helped the old woman into my room, she sat on my bed, no one had ever sat on my bed. Helen introduced Margaret. She looked nervous, looked out the window. She looked down at my books, a smile came over her face at the cover. She pointed at the mountain, she said, "Mount Cook." I turned the page, she pointed at the photograph of a waterfall, she said, "Milford Sound." I flipped, she called out the names as we went on. She gave me more information about every page. I drank it up, her words were music in my ears. I kept asking her if these places really did exist. She kept telling me, "They do, oh yes, they do!" At the end of the book, we both fell backward, exhausted. We lay on our backs, we stared at the ceiling, both of us had pictures in our mind playing behind our foreheads. They were pictures I wanted to make real, that I wanted to see, to touch. Margaret smiled at me, she left me alone. I went to sleep, I could not sleep. I flipped through the book one more time by the moonlight.

The next day I ate my kiwi sitting next to Margaret. I never noticed her during lunch before. I noticed a lot of things I didn't before. She told me stories about growing up in New Zealand. She told me about her hometown by the ocean. The town was called Greymouth. She told me about secret beaches, places where it felt like no one else had ever been. She told me about the people, about the sheep, about having to move away. She wished she could go home, she could not. I asked her why, she did not want to tell me. Whenever I asked her, she only sighed, shrugged. I learned many things about New Zealand from her.

I was not sleeping much during the nights. Sleep did not come. There was a voice speaking to me, that other voice, it told me something else. It was forming a plan with me, it was telling me strange things like I could go to New Zealand, I could see the places in the book, it was a possibility. These were foreign thoughts for me. I argued with this new voice. It told me it was trying to help me, it was trying to push me to go places where I would be happy, where I would become aware of the world around me, see it for what it was, drink it up, take the pieces I liked, drop them in the In Box, keep them close, fill myself up with mountains, lakes, oceans, beaches. Take it all in, all of it, grab on to it, do not let go.

Chapter Five

The plan formed in my head while I tried to sleep in my hospital bed, out for walks through the forest, when I touched the trees. The trees provided strength. The plan developed underwater when I swam in the lake, when I sat at the edge of the lake, looked at the water, when I ate my kiwis, talked with Margaret, learned more about New Zealand. Kept it all to myself, did not tell Helen, did not tell Jimmy, did not tell the doctors. A beard started growing in, my hair grew long. The doctor became suspicious about my new appearance. I told him I was going for something different, I was changing so much on the inside that I wanted to change on the outside. He seemed satisfied with this answer, did not ask me about it again, only complimented my beard as it grew.

The only one I told was my sister. She visited me, I asked her to go out for a walk with me. I was nervous about telling her, worried about asking for help, she had already done so much. I could not do this without her. She knew I was nervous, knew I needed to tell her something. It was time for me to leave this place, but the doctor didn't necessarily agree. I wanted to know what she honestly thought, if she disagreed with me, I would talk no further.

She was silent for a long time. She nodded her head finally, smiled. As we went through the plan, she never second-guessed me, never suggested something else, never attempted to persuade me towards another direction. Only nodded, added the odd suggestion and told me she would provide all the help she could. She would be happy to help me, talked about how this was a new step towards a new life, one where I would be independent, where I would live life on my own terms, see the world, live inside of it, try to find happiness somewhere far away. So relieved, I thought she would have tried to talk me out of it, but I should have known better, should have known she would only encourage me. I told her all about New Zealand, she saw how the mountains and the lakes and the ocean lit up my eyes. There was no way I could not go.

From then on we were in constant contact daily through the telephone. My sister visited me every week, we walked out into the woods, and we went over the developments of the plan. She brought me requested items such as maps and books and information I needed to make the plan fully complete. With the help of my sister, we mapped out the transit system of the city, how I would reach the airport, where the locker would be, the new documents that I would need, plane tickets. We then mapped out New Zealand, when I would arrive, trains, cars, ferries, my destination, the apartment. We worked together, the two of us, two siblings lost in the world with no one but each other.

With everything organized, we picked a date, settled on a month from our last meeting. My sister needed to set some things up through her contacts. She would give me the go ahead, then I would be on my own.

The last time I saw her was out in the woods. We were going over the flight and how I needed to make a connection in Los Angeles. We went over it three times. I folded the maps and papers, put them inside my shirt to bring back into the hospital. She grabbed my arm, spun me around to face her. She looked into my eyes, said, "This is it, we will not see each other for a while. The past few weeks have made me very happy. I can see that you will be fine. I will admit, although I might not have shown it, I was hesitant at first. I have to be honest and say I doubted whether you were ready for this, but I am only disappointed in myself for these thoughts of doubt. These past few weeks have made me happy because we are brother and sister again. We have become two people with a common goal, working together, getting to know each other again. I spent so many hours sitting, standing and watching you but feeling like I had been seeing someone else. I did not know this person, but you have come back, you have surfaced, and it is your own doing. To say that I am proud of you is an understatement. You have grown so much, you have taken your life back with both hands. It is yours now, you should do with it what you want, push ever forward, go find what you are looking for. There are so many things out there for you to experience and you will experience them as a new person, someone who has the opportunity to feel emotions like they are new. I hope you will find what you are looking for. A fire has been ignited under you, I hope you never allow the flame to burn out. I hope you always keep moving, always grow more, learn what it is that you want and get it. The only thing I can say is when you get it, grab on to it with both hands, hold it close and never let it go."

We walked through the hospital, out the front door to her car. We hugged, she held me closer than before, whispered in my ear, "Good luck. We will be reunited sooner than you think." She got in her car, rolled the window down, smiled at me. She had tears in her eyes, but they did not fall down her cheeks. She pulled out, I watched the car speed away. Before she got too far away, her arm appeared out the window, her hand turning into a fist. I held my arm up, turned my hand into a fist. I wondered if she saw me. The car turned the corner.

Alone.

One more month left.

That night I was going over a book about the South Island in New Zealand when a piercing scream came from the other side of the room. For a minute I thought it was the voice, someone screaming at me. I jumped out of bed, the book fell face down on the floor. The curtain flung open. Jimmy was out of bed standing staring at me like he was waiting for me. His eyes were not his own, he stepped closer to me, shouted, "We've got to get outta here they're going to kill us, come on." He quickly walked over to the door, hid beside the doorway, peeked outside. I told him, "Who is going to kill us?" He was only half listening to me, he continued, "The hallway is empty. Now's our chance, come on." He had something in his hand, too dark to tell what. When I stepped towards him, he spun his head around, "Don't come any closer to me. We leave together but stay away." He turned back towards the door, I asked, "Who are you looking for?" Jimmy turned towards me, "You're one of them, is that it? You're with them. You're one of the ghosts, the ones that skin you alive, they take your skin, leave you in a cell, cut your face off, your nose, ears then leave you bleeding on the floor. They do it nicely, laugh, joke, they take your fingernails off, cut your fingers off." He heard a noise in the hallway, "Shit they are coming, I cannot let them get me." Jimmy ran to the window, wrenched the pole holding the curtains right out of the floor. He swung it like an axe, smashing the window. He stood up on the window sill, I tried to grab him before he jumped. Hospital orderlies entered the room. I pointed to the window. I glanced out the window with them. We were on the third floor, Jimmy was on the ground, he looked shaken up but not hurt. He stood up, looked at us, gave us the finger, ran into the forest – towards my forest. The orderlies ran out of the room. I looked down, wondered if I would hurt myself. I jumped out of the window, tried to soften the blow to my legs, rolled on the ground, checked my body, nothing seemed broken, I ran after Jimmy.

I knew these woods better than anyone. If anyone found him, it would be me. At the border of the forest, I listened, heard footsteps ahead of me. Ran, stopped again, listened again. Mumbling coming from somewhere, and I ran in the direction of the mumbling. We went deep into the forest. It was dark outside, it was dark in here, darker than I thought it would be. The forest was different than in the day, but my legs knew the way, they knew every inch. I pursued Jimmy through the forest, heard him shouting the word Maggot.

Jimmy was running fast. I finally caught up to him, found him crouched, breathing heavily under a tree. He looked at me, he was too tired to struggle, would not budge, would not stand up. I said, "Jimmy, do you want to see something special, something no one else has seen?" This perked him up. He stood, led him to the lake in the middle of the forest. The stars pressed down on us from above, felt as though you could reach up, touch them, put one in your pocket, save it for later.

We sat beside the water, he put the metal staff on the ground beside him. I picked it up, put it on the other side of me. We just sat there, watched the light breeze press on the lake, morphing the reflection of the stars. Nothing was said. He looked down at the ground. Tears in his eyes. Not usual tears, these tears had weight to them. The kind of tears that accumulated after years. I just nodded my head, told him I understood, that I knew what his tears were made out of. I put my arm around him. We sat there quietly. I only wanted Jimmy to get those tears out of him, to make his own Outbox, get that crap out of his system.

We sat for a long time when the orderlies found us. Jimmy stood up, scared. I held my arms out, told them, "No! No! Wait!" They did not listen to me, tackled Jimmy, tackled me, shoved my face into the ground, put plastic rope around our wrists. They stood us up, marched us through the forest. This place had been soiled. Not by Jimmy, he was welcomed, but because of the orderlies, because they created a form of chaos. They did not listen, did not want to hear, they only reacted. I glanced at Jimmy, he would not look at me. I made eye contact with each one of them, they could not meet my eyes. When we reached the hospital, the doctor waited at the door. Helen was beside him, the doctor shook his head at us, looked at me, I glared right back. I shrugged my shoulders. They separated us. I was able to get some things from my room, picked up the book that fell to the floor, some pages were bent. I would be sleeping somewhere else until the window was fixed.

They put me in a room, straps on my wrists, ankles. I tried to reason with them that this was not necessary, that I never had these on before. No one talked to me. I asked about Jimmy, no one told me anything.

After a day in the straps, a day where I did not move, no tears came to my eyes. Only images of New Zealand filled my head. My body was useless, trapped. My mind took me to places I would soon be. I stood on top of mountains, swam in oceans, I was far away from this place. I was not a violent person, the only violence was towards myself. I never really saw the pressures that the people working in this hospital had to deal with. The threat that any one of us patients could fly off the handle, see things that were not there, try to defend ourselves. Their only recourse was to sometimes use violence against violence. I never knew what happened to Jimmy, never saw him again. No one talked to me, only said he was transferred.

The doctor asked me if I was trying to escape, if I was trying to get out, if this was something Jimmy and I planned. I did not answer, only thought of when I was leaving. Counting the days. I tried to act normal so they would take the straps off, so they would let me stay in my room again, let me take my walks, eat my kiwis. My thought pattern was disrupted. A routine was developed, the routine was now broken. I had to deal with it, reasoned with myself that this was proper training. Once I was outside these walls, I would be in a constant state of change, that I must adapt. I told the doctor I would not speak to anyone but Helen. She came right away, I explained what happened, told her the truth. Jimmy was only protecting himself, that I had nothing to do with it, I was just trying to help him. Helen knew I would not lie to her. I felt terrible for Jimmy, felt awful for telling the truth, but I needed to get out. It was time. I needed to focus on the plan, and the plan did not have the extra difficulty of being in straps.

The window was fixed, Jimmy's bed was empty, neatly made. I sat on my bed, looked out the window. Looked at the calendar, counting the days. That night I prepared the envelopes, each one numbered, each one with the specifically required contents. In a few days, I received the final package from my sister that had the key to the locker. Placed it in the envelope, hid the envelopes in the space between the mattress and the box spring. Ate my kiwis every day, felt them go down into my stomach. I was allowed to take my walks. For the first few days, I had an escort of an orderly. I joked with him, was friendly, he must have reported that I was no harm because I stopped needing a companion.

The voice over my shoulder was there, always there. I ignored it. The incident with Jimmy gave me strength somehow. I knew that I could fool them, knew that I had pulled all kinds of power from the trees and from the lake. The voices from the hospital died down, did not bother me as much. I just had no room in my head for all of them. The photographs of mountains and oceans were burned on the inside of my forehead, pushed out all unnecessary thoughts. The voice over my left shoulder tried to squeeze in there, commented on what I was thinking, on what I was planning on doing, but I just did not want to hear it anymore.

Two experiences happened which sealed the deal for me. The first was an appointment with the doctor. I was summoned to his office, sat in the chair across from him. He did not look at me, he was reading a file, I assumed my file. He finally looked at me, smiled, it was not a real smile. He asked me questions, talked about me as though I was not there, like I was another person. In the end, he said he was assessing whether I was ready to be released into a halfway house, a place where I could start reintegrating myself back into the world. I laughed out loud. I was thinking of New Zealand, he was thinking a halfway house. He thought I was laughing at something else. He closed the file, looked at me sternly. He said he does not think I am ready to leave, that I have not recovered to his satisfaction. He told me I was doing well, but that the Jimmy incidence had given him pause. After barely looking at me, he thanked me very much, said I could go. I laughed at this, walked out because I thought to myself how he just told me I may go now. These were words that had more meaning than he could ever know. I walked back to my room, understood his perspective. I just did not agree with it, knew he had a job, that was all he was doing, but I knew in my heart I was ready to leave.

My heart and my mind were connected in ways I never thought possible. Information flowed freely from one to the other. They had conversations I could not follow.

They were guiding me in directions that contradicted everything the voice over my shoulder advised. They spoke to each other of peace, of living a life where I was not afraid, a place where I used fear as an instrument to face new situations instead of succumbing to fear. A fear that made my shoulders sag, where all I wanted was to lay in bed, curl up in the fetal position and never wake. I walked down the hallway, repeated the doctor's mantra: You may go now. He said many things to me in that office, but in my head, I got his blessing. I changed his words, forgot that someone else told them to me. I turned them to my words, repeated to myself - I may go now I may go now I may go now.

The second experience was during a walk. After my kiwi, I stepped outside, it was overcast. Thick, fluffy grey clouds packed into the sky, blocking out the sun, the ground in the forest slightly moist, springy. I touched the trees, there was a pulse in the air that translated in the roots. I came to the area where I found Jimmy that day. There was a flattened bush. Some branches were broken, I cleaned it up, tried my best to fix the bush. I even tried to give it some of my strength, so maybe it would grow again and be healthy as it was before. I continued on to the lake. A fog settled in by the time I got to the water. The air was dense, difficult to see in front of me. The condensation was focused on top of the water, I could not see the other side. It made the lake look like it went on forever. I stood at the edge of the water. I stuck my hand in the fog, my hand disappeared. I pulled my hand back. Immediately took my clothes off, walked over to the tree with the branches, over the water. I climbed the tree, balanced on the branch. My body disappeared into the fog. I jumped off the branch into the mist, it was so thick it held me in the air. I was stuck in it like a giant spider's web. I rolled my arms around in circles, kicked my feet, moved through the fog, suspended in the air. It was like flying but very slowly. I floated towards the centre of the lake, looked all around, could not see the land. I could not see any trees. I could not see the water below me. Only the fog. I felt like my mind had spilled out of my ears. My mind was fog, heavy fog that you could not see through, a fog that had taken over my life, that made things so difficult for me to see. I wanted it to clear, wanted it to finally go away. I closed my eyes, thought about the fog going away. I felt something warm on my face, opened my eyes. A beam of sunlight was shooting through the fog, hitting me right in the face. I focused my thoughts on the fog clearing, and the sun became warmer, brighter. The sun pushed through the clouds, the fog dissipated. I fell into the cold water. I immediately broke back through the surface. The sky was clear, there were still some clouds, but they had moved on somewhere else. I waded in the water, convinced myself this was all just a coincidence. Maybe someone was trying to tell me something? Perhaps not, but I got the message. I could control my mind. My mind was the only one I had. I must maintain the connection to my heart, continue the dialogue. I finished my swim, felt light, my thoughts were clear, my body agreed with me.

Only a few more days to go. A model patient. Ate my kiwis, walked my walks, spoke with the doctor, made Helen laugh. At night I got ready, everything was in place. I was waiting for the signal from my sister that all was good on her end. The signal came in the mail, it was a postcard. There was nothing written on the postcard. It was sent from New Zealand. The address was the apartment I would be staying at. On the front of the postcard was a mountain, at the foot of the mountain lay a great beach with the ocean beyond it as far as you could see. I smiled, knew it was time. Two more days. They would be long days, but I would be patient. I had a goal in mind. My body pulsed, my bones wanted to jump out of my skin. I relaxed, got everything calm. I put the postcard with the other contents between the mattress and the box spring.

A vivid dream happened during the night. A voice called out to me, I almost did not recognize it as the voice over my left shoulder. It was talking from far away, threatening to go to the doctors and to Helen and tell them what I had been planning. I pushed it down and away. I woke up by being pushed off the bed by an orderly. Stumbled to the ground. Confused, I looked in horror as he lifted the mattress, threw it to the side, grabbed the envelopes. He held them up while looking at me. His eyebrows arched towards the sky. Without taking his eyes off me, he held them out. The doctor came into view, took the envelopes, ripped them open, found the key. He asked what all this was for, yelled at me. Helen stood beside him, she looked at the floor, she could not look at me. Another orderly grabbed me, pulled me from the room. Dragged along the ground, the floor covered with broken glass. The orderly's shoes cracked on the glass-covered linoleum floor. The door at the end of the hallway disappeared, looked like a black hole. I started screaming. It was darker than I had ever seen before. Scared. I had been able to take myself away from the darkness, I was being pulled back into it. They pulled, I tried to fight, but I had no strength. My blood from the broken glass was left behind, I was pulled into the doorway, engulfed in the darkness.

Woke up.

My body covered in sweat. I rolled on to the floor at some point in the night. The voice was there with me, the voice told me I would fail, they would catch me. I would never be allowed to leave these walls. It called me names. I climbed back on to the bed, pulled the covers up over me, even though I was boiling hot. Closed my eyes, pushed the voice away. It was persistent, it would not leave me be. I asked it to go. I only had two more days, just let me be, please. The voice knew it had me on the run now. It was strong tonight. It had been saving its strength to make this appearance right before I left. It wanted me to stay because here it ruled me. I could not get from under its thumb. I pushed it away, imagined I was standing on a beach. There was a small rowboat, I got in the boat, left the voice on the beach. I rowed with all my strength, pushed my muscles, did not know how long it would take me to reach the other side, but I just knew I needed to get away from it. Pushed, pulled. I somehow fell asleep drifting in the rowboat in the middle of the ocean where it was quiet, free from the voice telling me I could not do what I had been dreaming of for so long.

I woke up, it was a bad day. I did not want to get out of bed. I wanted tomorrow to come. I had discovered the great idea of tomorrow. I looked forward to it but not right now. At this moment I had to focus all my strength and all my energy on getting out of bed. I tried three times, on the third time I sat up, rolled my legs around the side, touched my feet to the ground. I got control of my breathing, it went in, and it went out. The voice was coming, I was too tired to listen. I hoisted myself on to my feet, walked across to the bathroom, looked at myself in the mirror. Dark circles surrounded my eyes. I tried to wash them off with water, they remained. My head was full of dark clouds, I tried to make the clouds go away, tried to reintroduce the mountains and the oceans. It took too much energy. Why was I feeling like this the day before I left? I would need all my strength tomorrow. I would need it all to push forward, to survive outside these walls.

The voice continued whispering. I closed my eyes, listened to what it said. Just the sound of it made me lean my back against the wall, weakened. I slid down the wall, sat on the floor, hung my head. I could not do this. I could not. I listened to it, felt my body sink closer and closer to the ground. I rested my cheek on the floor, I just wanted to sleep, wanted to listen to the voice, forget all about these plans. I was stupid to think

I could actually do it.

I heard that other voice. It started small. It was far away. It started in my feet, raced through my legs, spoke to all my insides, whispered into the ear of my heart, traveled up to my brain. The voice told me essential words. It told me I could do it. This other voice said, Sit up! I listened to it, opened my eyes. I placed my hands on either side of my head, pushed up with my hands, raised my head. It still hung, but there was new strength in there. I pushed my shoulders back, the new voice told me, Stand up! I slowly stood up, struggled to get my balance. It told me, Look in the mirror! I looked in the mirror, the bags under my eyes were gone. I breathed deep, continued on, I could do it.

I got dressed, went down, ate my kiwi. It was the best kiwi I had eaten since I arrived here in this hospital. After lunch, I visited Margaret. Sat next to her in front of the window. Put my hand on her shoulder, felt the energy pulsing from her. We sat in silence until I said, "Thank you!" She looked into my eyes, I felt she knew what I was going to do. She smiled a big smile. I had never seen her smile, I told her, "You have the most beautiful smile I have ever seen. You should use it more often." This made her smile wider. She looked down at her hands in her lap, embarrassed. I stood up, she called after me, she said, "Good luck!" I waved to her, I gave her a majestic bow, one reserved for kings and queens.

I returned to my room. The voice over my shoulder had been there all day. He was still there, but I pushed him down. I went for my walk. I said to the trees, Goodbye! I said to the lake, Goodbye! I thanked them for the strength, for empowering me. I told them I would be back. I lay in bed, pulled the covers over my head. I felt I could not keep a thought for more than a second. One appeared, and another one was ready to push it out of the way. I went over the plan at least twenty times. Everything was in place. Only a few more hours until I left. There was no chance I would sleep until then. My mind raced, it thought about all of the places I would see, all of the things that I would experience. I hungered for it, my stomach rumbled at the thought. Everything was connected. My heart, my mind, my body. All ready. The voice told me I was not prepared. I ignored it. I had other things to think about. I had another voice to listen to. I changed the dial like a radio. I watched the stars through my window. I imagined I could grab them, put them in my pocket, save them for later.

Chapter Six

Helen checked on me for the last time in the middle of the night, left my door open. She trusted me. After she left, I dramatically removed the bedspread to reveal that I had my clothes on already. I was clever that way. Nothing else was going with me. Every one of my possessions would remain as they were, they only lacked an owner. I felt nothing, they were things that had comforted me in the past but no more. I said GOODBYE to my books. I said GOODBYE to my music. I said GOODBYE to the bed I slept in for years. A bed that I had twisted and turned on top of and thought thoughts I didn't want to consider anymore. I made the bed, I respected the bed that provided me with rest when the voices were asleep.

The hallway was empty, the plans unfolding in my favour from the start. Should I thank God? He deserted me a long time ago. There was a time I talked to him directly, or so I thought. He didn't say much except, "HELLO! Remember to floss after eating!" I said, "What are you talking about, is that it?" He repeated himself, winked at me, the wink patronizing the way you'd expect from God. He never spoke to me again, I never talked to him again - the feeling mutual.

Down the hallway to the stairwell – this was a low-security area. The staff trusted me, we were usually on lockdown in our rooms anyway. Padding lightly towards the end of the hallway, quietly down the stairs, stopped. Voices. Not THOSE voices, actual real-life voices. The night shift nurses, one of them Helen. I could pick her voice out of a crowd of shouting people. One more time I got to hear her voice. Listening from above, Helen and the other night shift nurse talked about a television show. They stopped at the floor below me and opened the door. The stairwell went quiet, not even the vibrations from their voices remained.

The ground floor – the tricky part. The anxiety of the ground floor turned the sound up in the back of my head, but by the Grace of God, it stayed to a low murmur. The sound I heard was fear and fear was only a feeling, and I could control my feelings. Pushed it down, pushed it out of my head, down down down through my spine and farted it out – a smelly, juicy one. The really smelly, juicy ones contained fear bubbles leaving my body.

Through the door to the hallway, I saw the security station, but before I broached that next level area of anxiety, the plan was to duck cat-burglar-like into the doctor's station. Ten steps to the doctor's station – HOLY SHIT – it was empty. The white doctor's coat was a good fit, I could have been a doctor in another life. In the small mirror on the inside of the locker, I could be a doctor right now. Well, smart guy, that was the plan. There was even a clipboard. This was all coming together better then even the Grace of God could've imagined. Large breath thinking about the security station – remembered to breathe. There goes another fart. Loud. Maybe too loud? Smells. God help who was coming in here on their break to eat.

Remember, walk with confidence. Walk like I belonged. I did belong but not in the way the rightful owner of this coat did. Another fart, made sure I put on the silencer.

The security station was encased in glass, the guard inside. Built into the desk were ten monitors showing different areas of the hospital. Hey, there I am on television! I should do something funny or at least wave but crushed this feeling, contained it, put the feeling away into my little box. The box was getting damn full, kept emptying but there continued to be sights I saw and sounds I heard that belonged inside it.

On the clipboard was my saviour: a pen. Deep

thoughts came over my eyes as I turned over a recent patient in my mind. That guy up in room 405, who couldn't stop farting and kept nattering on about his boxes, he seemed to be getting better but I still UP THE MEDS with a stroke of my pen. On the television monitor as I walked by, there was a doctor on the monitor – hey that's me – even I was convinced. The security guard was reading a magazine on trout fishing, an advertisement on one page claimed The Best Bass Fishing Around, and there was a picture of a standup bass guitar jumping out of a lake. A laugh was squashed, but half a chuckle left my lips. He did not look up from reading about the best bass fishing around. As the corner was rounded, I gave him the gift of a nice juicy fart. Fear was not coming out of my ass, but victory. Victory smelled even worse than fear. I haven't figured out why yet, it just did.

Down the long country road away from the hospital, I stopped when far enough away to look back and said GOODBYE to the hospital. These walls were kind to me, but I hit a plateau that no doctor would want to admit and it was time to move onwards and upwards.

The bus stop stood at the crossroads. The bus schedule was amazingly accurate on the internet – yes, we had access to computers. Various social media platforms are a healthy way to communicate with the outside world. People didn't have to look us in the eyes. Schedules studied, the route imprinted on my brain, I still went over my plan as I stood waiting in the pitch darkness for bus 405. What a coincidence! The lights of the hospital visible, which should technically create anxiety, but strangely there was none.

The choice to wait at this bus stop seemed like such a small decision, but it was my decision. I was the boss here, and this trip was all about choice. There was not much choice over the last few years, only feelings of being trapped, tied up, boxed in, locked up, turned around. A through-line towards my goal was visible, it was MY goal and MINE alone and NOBODY else's.

That all being said, it was still damn cold outside – that's what you got when the plan was formed in the winter. What I was wearing could not be considered adequately dressed: a dark brown pair of slacks, my lucky blue button-down shirt, light brown zip-down sweater. The only luggage I had was my shoulder bag that was appropriately around my shoulder.

The bus finally came, on the side, it said it was a hybrid electric bus. Oh, have times changed. There was a pause before the doors opened, a pause like the world had stopped. At least, my world. This was the point of no return, a breath, a sigh, running between the spaces of the wind – the wind which howled furiously before now stopped, took a break, opened up a time capsule for me to review my choice to leave this place. My breathing stopped with the wind, held my breath, my mind clicked, someone inside me said, *Do not get on that bus*. The voice told me I could not do it, said I should sneak back into the hospital. Above I omitted the fact that I was still wearing the doctor's coat and holding the clipboard. It would be easy to sneak back in and crawl under the covers of my bed in room 405. The voice shouted, but I chose to squash it down, sent it backside and out of my body.

A hydraulic noise shifted inside the door, rattled across my brain but delayed, did not yet register. After a moment or ten, the driver stared at me. I remembered the other element of my plan – the essential part – the part where I acted NORMAL. I flashed him a smile – not just any smile, but a winning smile – one that said: I am sorry sir for the delay, just remembering if I locked my front door or not!

Everything was prepared in small envelopes – I wondered what these small type of envelopes were for, now I know. Envelope number one was labeled PILL #1. The kicker: it was not a pill. Not to brag, but it was a coding system developed if someone found my stash. Failure surely would come with succinct envelopes that said something like BUS FARE TO SNEAK OUT OF HOSPITAL.

Emptied the contents of the envelope into my hand, it should have the exact change. I was an old woman counting her pennies at the cash register. Dumped the change in the slot and smiled and almost felt like he should be congratulating me. He didn't, so instead, I congratulated myself. The driver handed me a transfer, all the places I could get to with this transfer! This thin piece of paper that most people chose to throw on the ground – I cherished it. Thanked it for transferring me from here to there. My ticket to freedom. The driver stared thinking I'm staring at him. He waited for me to move, pointed down at the thick white line on the floor of the bus, motioned towards a small sign that read, PLEASE STAY BEHIND THE WHITE LINE. My eyes rolled in an exaggerated smile and slowly shook my head and shrugged my shoulders. Maybe I was laying it on a bit thick, but I chose to spread it that way.

A few steps into the bus and now behind the white line. The driver did not acknowledge me crossing the finish line; instead, he pulled the bus on to the street, and we were off. Disappointing and exhilarating at the same time.

Three desperate people were riding the bus with me tonight. The kind of people that needed to ride the bus at this time must be insomniacs in need of company.

Whenever I couldn't sleep - and that was many times - I dropped things to make noises, so Helen or someone else had to see what was up. I started discussions about refugee rights or the War on Terror, except if John the Nurse appeared. If John the Nurse was on duty and came in the room, I pretended I was asleep, and if he woke me, I'd swear the noise wasn't me.

I was standing and staring again, I must remember not to do this. Although nobody was looking at me, they were in their own worlds. Did they hear voices? Were there people inside them that were not them? Could people tell when they looked at me? Did they know that something was not right about me? Maybe I was just like everyone else, maybe I'd fit right in?

Snapping out of my staring fit, I walked to the back, sat down, looked at the other passengers who had not acknowledged me. One part of me wanted to jump up and shout to make them look at me, but the central part of my plan was to be stealth. Some airplanes used these kinds of maneuvers to go undetected. Part of my plan was to be invisible to other people around me so they didn't know and couldn't possibly figure out that they're looking at someone who had sneaked out of a hospital. So when people from the hospital came looking for me, they would come to dead-end after dead-end because nobody remembered me. Imagine: moving through the world invisible and unseen and completely anonymous!

One passenger was an old man who needed a shave. His white hair formed a crown around the top of his head, his head covered in spots. Although I was looking at the back of his head, I felt his eyes darting back and forth watching, looking for something outside. Maybe he was looking for a lost dog? Maybe his memory was gone – he could not remember which stop to get off – and he was worried, lost, needed help? He was a stubborn war veteran, liked to live with pain and pride and wouldn't ask anyone for help. I leaned into the aisle to take a better look at him. Totally wrong. His eyes were closed, he was sleeping, searching for something in his sleep.

The second person on the bus was a woman. About thirty-five, but I didn't want to say anything definite as I was totally wrong about the old man. Long beautiful hair, she stared at the floor, clutched on her lap a giant purse that a standup lamp could fit into. Was she coming home from the house of her lover? Maybe she was coming back from work after the late shift at a hospital? Not the one I was coming from because I would have recognized her. Perhaps she worried about her eight-year-old daughter that she had to leave alone at home? Whichever one it was, she looked worried but were her worries about where she was coming from or where she was going?

The third was a twitchy young fellow who was definitely awake. He had a drink in a brown paper bag - that was an actual thing that people did - and took a swig of it every ten seconds. I knew this because I had been timing him. His other hand clutched the handle on the back of the seat in front of him, clasped it so hard his knuckles were white. The dark circles under his eyes told a story about long nights – too many long nights – staying up through the hours when everyone was sleeping, becoming out of synch with those around him, increasingly becoming paranoid, hearing voices inside his head that told him to do things he did not want to do. He looked panicky, looked like he didn't know what to do. There was confusion behind his eyes, he was afraid his thoughts had steadily been breaking down, he was losing touch with reality only to create his own reality, a world where fears ran wild in the veins. He clawed at his veins, ripped open his skin leaving sores – out out out fear leave this body. He couldn't deal with it, so he started taking drugs, first just smoking a little bit here and there and then chemicals, trying to numb the pain, to silence the voices but they came on stronger and more powerful. They were no longer in my head, they were right beside me, right at my shoulder whispering into my ears, they told me – WAIT – that was me I'm thinking about!

I fell back into myself. Smiled to nobody, rolled my eyes, slowly shook my head. Shrugged my shoulders as if to say, Where did that come from?

The twitchy man rang the bell, jumped up, exited the bus. My stop next and it was my time to ring the bell. Ready at the doors, I decided to make some noise but had nothing to drop, so I did some fake coughing that sounded real. The old man woke up, and I asked him if this was his stop. He looked at me like I was crazy, it was like I woke him up from the most peaceful rest ever. Whatever old man, I was out the door.

The bus was getting stuffy. I didn't belong there with those people. My next bus was across the street, literally - it sat idling like it was waiting just for me. I must pay more attention because I was almost hit by a car when crossing the street. Tires squealed. I locked eyes with the eyes behind the wheel. This driver had angry bloodshot eyes. Her eyes did not even have enough energy to move, they stayed on me, I was lost in them. There were many eyes like them in the hospital, when people were breaking up, cracking up. When they had enough, and their mind finally snapped and said GOODBYE! I stepped away from the car slowly, tried to break her gaze, but she kept the tractor beam on. I heard more hydraulics, the doors closed, I summoned the courage and broke eye contact.

Running for the bus, I put my hand into the door, it closed around my forearm, and I imagined the driver continuing on with my arm in the door. I would have to run fast if this was the case. The door opened, thank you for my arm back. Stepping up into the bus, shaking my head as if I said: Just another commuter trying to get to work on time at 3:30 in the morning! I showed the driver my transfer, he did not look at me. I wanted his approval, but he only closed the door and drove on. To get his attention, I purposely dropped the transfer and picked it up to show him. Made a big show of it. He still ignored me, so I pushed it into his face, he pushed my hand away. I must admit that this was creating a distraction, which was both unsafe and unfair. At least he saw it. My watch said I was right on time. The bus was empty.

The roads gave way to cement. No airplanes visible yet but I heard them, flying overhead and crisscrossing each other without knowing how close they were to complete and utter disaster. We passed an area where several highways all merged together, and in between them there was a large patch of grass with gravestones. Which came first: the roads or the tombstones? The people there must not rest peacefully, even at this time of the night there were cars, trucks, headlights, horns, airplanes. Only wicked people must be buried there because I heard they don't get any rest.

At the first stop off the highway, a woman got on the bus. Or I should have said her bags got on the bus and then her. She must have had ten bags – okay not ten bags – but a lot of bags and they were all huge and what the hell was inside? The bus was empty, but she sat in the seat right in front of me. She had built a fort around us with her bags, they kept falling over as the bus stopped and started. She kept looking at me rolling her eyes and giving me a smile – did she know that I knew it was not a sincere smile? Maybe it was, I had been wrong before.

"Excuse me," she said.

"Yes," I said, I thought I said that, pretty sure that's what I said.

"Do you know which terminal I go to?" The woman showed me her ticket. Her first name was Helen – how fitting, of course, her name was Helen! For a moment I remembered Helen the nurse asking me about things in my life, about people who cared about me. We always had conversations with depth. Someone inside told me the Helen beside me was asking a question right now in the present tense. As in, on the bus. She was looking to me for an answer, she was waiting, but soon the expression would change to the squinty-eyed look. I didn't want our relationship, whatever infantile stage it was in, to go in that direction. The destination on the ticket said Amsterdam. Amsterdam is the capital of the Netherlands, but I had no idea which terminal she needed to go to get there.

Wait a second, there was more than one terminal? Which terminal was I leaving from?

My eyes narrowed as I explored her ticket. This was getting critical, I really needed to say something.

Handing the ticket back to her, I thoughtfully replied, "I'm sorry, I can't say." She said, "Thanks anyway."

There was a lull in our conversation, I was not sure where we were to go from here. This was my first interaction with someone outside of the hospital for a long time, and I wanted to make the best of it. The practice was needed as well, this was something that would happen often.

"Where are you going?" I damn well knew where she was going.

"Amsterdam, you?" She smiled without judgment as she answered.

"New Zealand."

"Wow."

Her wow sounded sincere, so I repeated back, "Wow." I widened my eyes for effect.

"What terminal are you going to?"

I took a deep breath, for some reason held it in, let out all the air, I said earnestly, "I'm not sure myself." There was a long pause, and she broke into laughter. Another break in the space-time continuum allowed me to take in the full effect of her laughter. Her laugh was just a healthy laugh, there was nothing special about it, but there was someone that was laughing with me, someone that was not laughing because they felt they had to. I have said something and her natural reaction was laughter and there was nothing more to it than that.

There was something that welled up in me, something deep down inside hiding away in my box. Something that should have never been placed in that box. I cursed the day that it was locked away. Something physically moved inside me that was unmovable. All the time I was bound up, I was lost, using up all my strength long ago, or so I thought. A great beast waking from a long slumber. Instead of forcing awake this beast and trying to use all my strength to move it, all along I should have made someone laugh – I mean really laugh - and the beast wouldn't have known what to do. It was coming up my spine and passing through my heart, my heart pounded in my ears, it was coming up my throat and heading towards my eyes. I didn't let it, not yet.

"Some of us like to travel light," I said. And I smiled, and she laughed again, and I almost lost control. "Some of us travel with everything they own," she countered.

That did it. I laughed, and I couldn't stop laughing, which graduated her laugh into a full-fledged laughing fit. I laughed from my chest – laughed from deep down in my belly. There was something inside not liking it, but I didn't care. She knew there was something wrong with me, but it did not matter because there was something wrong with her. We were just two eccentrics sitting on a bus in the early morning understanding that we were not alone – maybe we were – but even if we were, it did not matter.

The driver looked at us through his mirror, what was he thinking? Most of me didn't care. I have worried, concerned, wondered what others have thought about me, but not today, not now, I didn't care, I just laughed.

She opened a bag, took out a giant hair dryer, we

laughed some more. She opened another bag, took out a book of CDs - CDS! Even I knew no one had CDs anymore. She pulled out Nirvana Nevermind.

"I haven't listened to this in ten years," she said. We laughed.

"Better not leave home without it," I said. "You might be in Amsterdam sitting by the water smoking a spliff thinking about your life when all of a sudden you have to listen to 'Smells Like Teen Spirit' as if it all depended on it." We laughed some more, she showed me her iPod, said she brought CDs as backups.

We arrived at the terminal she thought was hers. I launched the bags one at a time out the door into her arms like we were tossing sandbags to quell a flood. We waved GOODBYE! I watched her through the window – I saw myself in the window – someone was smiling back at me. Hey, it's me! Mine was the next terminal, at least I thought this was the one. Strike that last sentence, I was sure of it because I was choosing to do something different now, I was making a choice to choose.

The terminal looked different from the last time I was here, although that was many years ago. The building was quiet. A man shined the floors with a machine. The machine was quiet, and the floors already looked clean. Must give him something to do this early in the morning.

A camera was in the corner watching. Someone inside me started chattering that I was being watched, had been observed ever since I left the hospital. My actions were being recorded, they knew my every move, they were waiting, biding their time until they caught me. They were just letting me think I was making the choices I was making, and that my life was my own when in reality they would catch me at the gate to board the airplane, "Okay, you've had your fun now back home with you." I wrapped that feeling tight, I told the voice telling me these things that nobody knew I was gone. I had a head start, I was making my own choices. Those thoughts went into a box – not my box mentioned earlier, another box. I wrote out an address, slapped the address on the box. There was a sticker on it that said AIRMAIL. It was put on a conveyor belt and a man who had calluses on his knuckles and thick gravelly skin from too many cigarettes and had lifted hundreds of boxes just like it, pitched it on to a cargo plane. The plane took off, the plane landed at the tip of South America to a place in a town that I saw a photograph of once. In the photograph, there was a sign, and the sign read: YOU HAVE REACHED THE END OF THE WORLD. And there – THERE – they had a big pile of boxes, they tossed my box on top of the heap and not a peep ever came from it again.

Once that was done, I farted out some more leftover fear. The hardest part was still to come, and I stepped on to the escalator to go up up up! This was the part that caused me worries, and I have not mentioned it because I had been so worried. It was good I had other things to worry about, so I didn't get bogged down with this one.

Envelope #2 read PILL #2. Part of my code. I didn't want it to read KEY TO STORAGE LOCKER WITH PLANE TICKET, PASSPORT AND MONEY TO ESCAPE THE COUNTRY. That would be a bit much. The storage lockers were on the second floor. It was tough to look around for suspicious people because it made me be the suspicious person. The envelope opened in my hands, and the key fell into my palm. The number was memorized - locker #405. Nice touch by my sister. She had a flair for the melodramatic. The key turned, it was actually turning. I pulled the door open, it actually opened. Inside was a small leather document case. It was mine. The cameras were watching me, I must have looked confident. Remembered to look like I belonged. I closed the door on the empty locker, the key remained and I said GOODBYE to the key. It had given me so much more then it had given other people, or maybe I was wrong, maybe it had given so much more than I imagined.

Up to the next floor, I entered a stall, locked the door and sat down. Inside the leather case, there was a plane ticket in a stranger's name. The name was PAUL DORE, and I wondered where in the hell she came up with that strange name. The destination on the ticket was first to Los Angeles, then on to Auckland. Auckland was at the top of the North Island of New Zealand. Two islands make up New Zealand: one is the North Island, and the other is the South Island. Practical names. I had studied maps, knew facts - anyone could ask me anything about New Zealand.

There was a striking resemblance between my sister and me as everything in the case was in an individual envelope. In the second envelope, there was Canadian money, in the third envelope American money, in the fourth envelope New Zealand money. In the middle of the New Zealand bills was a tiny window that you could see through. The fifth envelope had a passport and a driver's license with my photograph on them, but with Paul Dore's name, which was now my name. The passport looked real to me, and the license seemed not bad. There was a sixth envelope, directions to where I would be staying. My sister had really taken care of things.

Outside, I told myself to look confident, but I was confident. It was not just a feeling I needed to feel, it was a feeling that I was actually feeling.

There was a small store, so I bought a tiny bottle of shaving cream and a razor. Back in the washroom, with the razor and shaving cream arranged on the side of the sink, I stopped, looked at myself. The beard started growing several weeks ago – it took a while. The beard was necessary, so I could shave it off, so if they posted my picture on the news or on the internet, and they used the most recent one available, it just so happened to coincide with the beard. They would have a photograph of someone with a beard – the beard was an integral part of the plan.

My eyes didn't look tired as they usually did. My hair needed cutting, but that was part of the plan as well. It was sticking up in the back, I licked the fingers on my right hand, tried to smooth it down, but the strands had their own idea. My nose, which I usually thought looked big, looked like it was getting smaller – maybe I was telling the truth more? Actually, I would be telling the truth less now that I was Paul Dore. Maybe my nose was shrinking because I was finally telling the truth to myself?

Shook all these thoughts off.

Lathered up the beard, I kind of liked it, but it had to go. Applied the shaving cream and shaved. Damn plastic razor scrapped across my face, it was a bit red at the end, but it would be okay. Without the beard, I was back to normal. Without the beard, I was Mr. Paul Dore.

I approached the check-in counter. I was strangely not nervous. There was no lineup, only an airplane representative half asleep at the wheel. I stood before her a few moments, she did not notice me. After dropping my leather case, she was still unaware of my presence. Coughing was my next go-to. It took three coughs, and on the third, she woke.

"Good morning!" I said a little too cheerily for so early in the morning. She held out her hand, I shook it, she shook her head, I shook my head, rolled my eyes and handed her my ticket.

"Any baggage?" The airplane representative asked.

"No," I replied truthfully.

"You're going a long way with no baggage."

Shrugged my shoulders, I mean, she was right. She shrugged her shoulders, I looked at the camera above her head. Someone inside was starting to tell me something – how did they get back from South America so soon? Shook it off, handed her my passport. She clicked some keys on the computer, handed back everything with a mint condition boarding pass. Inside there was another voice, but this voice was shouting good things like HORRAY and WELCOME TO NEW ZEALAND, MR. DORE! The airline representative returned her head on to her hand, went back to sleep. I winked at the camera – this might be a bit much but what the hell?

In the security area, my change went in a small plastic receptacle which looked like something from the hospital that you peed into except this one was rectangular and might be hard to manage for something like that. The security guard checked my boarding pass, nodded as he gave it back. The metal detector remained silent. ALL CLEAR I wanted to say but didn't.

Here I was at the gate that corresponded to the one on the plane ticket. I was early, and I sat not too close but not too far. There were cameras all over this place, so I sat off to the side holding my boarding pass in my hands. I clutched it, grasped it, the pass was my pass to the other side of the world. Fatigue was coming, but I was still wired and kept my eyes peeled for suspicious activity. Nothing happened. There was no one around, and I was bored with apprehension.

A gate agent sat behind the desk beside the gate. She typed into a computer and put her mouth to a microphone at her side. Over the loudspeaker: "Paul

Dore, please see gate attendant."

My blood pressure rose, gas lowered. I didn't know what to think. There was no one around. Maybe they were hiding, perhaps they were waiting? Maybe they thought it would be funny to have me walk right into their arms? Well, if this were the end, I would go down fighting.

I flashed a smile, a big smile, said, "I am Paul Dore."

"Good morning, Mr. Dore," she said.

"Is it?"

"Well, actually for you, yes. I asked you here because there is a problem with your ticket." My face dropped. The look I was going for was normal like this happened on all my business trips.

"We double booked your ticket to Auckland," she said. "We hope to rectify it by bumping you up to first class."

I said nothing for a while. I looked around. I knew she was waiting for a response. "All the way to New Zealand?"

She merely said, "Yes, of course."

My smile was genuine, and a little confused. She did the paperwork and told me that I had access to the first class lounge. I could go there now, and I could go there in Los Angeles. I headed to the lounge, thinking it was a joke, sure this was where they were going to grab me.

There were double doors, the doors opened inward, there was another attendant, I showed her my ticket, she unveiled her arm in presentation as though she was showing a new refrigerator to a contestant on a game show. Inside, the lounge was almost empty, food everywhere and hunger hit me suddenly. Gigantic plush chairs bordered the room, and a full bar was available even at this time of the morning. I poked my head into the washroom to find a shower, which I used to scrub behind my ears. Wearing a robe and slippers, I grabbed some food – croissant, eggs, bacon, fruit. Downed a coffee, drank tea, ate more, watched television. My flight number was called. My flight was going to take off but not without me.

Back to the gate, I was a bit tipsy due to all the food but that's okay, it helped take the edge off. This was where they will grab me.

On the ramp I stopped, I took in all the air I could, held my breath, looked around, let the air out, took a step and no alarms went off. Took another step and everything seemed fine.

The tunnel was attached like a giant suction cup to the plane – the air was different. The suction had changed the pattern of airflow, it stopped, and when it stopped you could peek between it and saw what was there, you saw if you are right or wrong or insane or sane or happy or sad or just plain fooling yourself. This was where it would happen: the pilots were not pilots, but police dressed as pilots. They would apprehend me in my sleep after I was comfortable in my seat with my eyes closed and they would toss me out the door when the plane was in the sky. The voice was back strong because this was the moment – this was where I stepped from one place to another. The air had been sucked out of this tunnel for me so I would recognize it, so I would see the choice I was making. I saw the damn choice – I didn't want to be reminded of some things. I punched the voice in the head, struggled with it, aware that those around me could not see the turmoil that churned in my head. They could not possibly comprehend what happened on the inside, but that did not make it any less real. I told myself to focus, told myself to put the voice in a full nelson, told myself to take a step so the air could flow once again, so the world could be right once again.

The flight attendant practically took my hand to show me my seat. The seat was huge. I tried it out – went backward and forwards. The flight attendant returned and offered orange juice or champagne. I took a tiny glass of orange juice, and I did a cheers to her, but I really cheered to myself. She smiled, and I smiled – was this the calm before the storm or just the calm? I looked out the window, and the maintenance guys were putting the last few touches on the plane – Fill it up! Everyone was on the plane, they slammed doors, the flight attendant filled my glass, and I cheers again.

Nobody was after me.

They did a final check, and so did I and we pulled away from the gate. They were coming – no they were not, yes they were, no they were not. We taxied out, stopped. They were coming to get me. The engines warmed up, got louder and louder. We screeched along the runway, going faster and faster. My heart went faster and faster – it was moving all over my body, thumping everywhere all at once. One wheel left the earth, the other wheels joined it and we were flying, we were in the air. The plane went up up up, and the world got smaller, and I said GOODBYE to everything that I had known for 33 years.

Everything was gone, I was starting new, leaving things behind I did not need, gaining everything I had always wanted, and nobody was out to get me. We went faster into the sky, we sliced through clouds – we were above the clouds! I got more orange juice, and I cheers again, and I downed the glass. Everything inside me dropped, I moved my heart back to my chest – it stopped thumping, it was going to sleep. I wanted to listen to it – I listened to my heart – that was all I wanted was to guide my life by what my heart thought, and it told me to sleep, that it needed rest, that I needed rest. It said I had done well today and that I was on my way. I let out a silent fart, a fart just for me and it smelled sweet. It was not the smell of fear it was not even the smell of victory it was something much better. It was a freedom fart. My heart was light, it was falling asleep, it said GOODNIGHT! It said to go to sleep, so I did.

I dreamt of tightness – no other way I could describe it. In the dream, it felt like there was a giant rope tied around my neck, the rope thick, coarse. Someone pulled on each end like they were playing tug of war. I could not see the people – their faces were blank. They pulled harder and harder, and my neck was getting squeezed, but I was not choking.

I have had this dream many times.

The first time I was very young, but something different happened – usually, that was it, that was the dream. That was all that happened, and I woke up, my neck was stiff, and I moved on with my life. Usually, my hands uselessly scratched at the rope wrapped around my neck, but this time they did something different. I grabbed the outstretched part of the rope, I clasped one hand on the rope shooting out from the front of my body and the other around behind my back, pulled with all my strength, and you know what happened next? The people holding the rope were pulled towards me, the tightness around my neck loosened for the briefest of moments and I pulled but my strength left me, and the rope went back to normal.

I woke up in the airplane in the sky somewhere above California. I looked out the window, I looked around at the other passengers. No one had thrown me out of the plane, no one had noticed me. I touched my neck, I usually woke up from this dream out of breath and unable to breathe but this time I felt good. I felt like I was fighting back, reclaiming something. I was struggling but for once on the winning side. In the washroom, in the mirror: I liked this person I saw more and more. There was an announcement to sit down, fasten your seatbelt, we will be landing in Los Angeles soon.

Los Angeles appeared sprawled out before me, went on forever and ever. It was daytime, and the light returned. It was sunny here, heard it was always sunny. The plane landed with a squeak – would it happen in

Los Angeles? Had they tracked me down? Was this where someone would grab me?

I took my possessions, left the airplane – the air was thick, I tasted it. The air tasted like a hamburger. I walked down the ramp and followed the signs for connecting flights. I swept the hallways and tunnels with my eyes, nobody looked at me twice. That did not mean anything, they could be letting me get this far to lower my guard.

Customs was the real test for Paul Dore. This was where it all went down or kept going. I tried to look uninterested in the process, as though I had done this many times before. Inside I was screaming, the voice was back, it must have taken a nap when I did. The voice was all rested up, it was following me to New Zealand, but maybe I could give it the slip.

Next in line, the voice got louder. There was a line on the floor that I waited behind until a passport officer was ready for me. I promised myself to leave the voice behind the line when it was my turn. The officer in front of me flipped a switch that turned a small blinking light on, indicating she was free when I could clearly see she was free. I stepped over the line, I left the voice behind. I presented Paul Dore: placed my passport on the tall table between us and I faced the woman who decided my fate. I slowly slid it towards her.

The officer picked the passport up, looked at it, looked at me, looked back at the passport, looked back at me. She asked, "Where are you coming from, sir?" I told the truth, I figured there was no use lying about this since that was where my plane came from. She was quiet for what seemed like a long time, I felt the voice itching to cross that line, I silently glared at it without her noticing. She asked totally monotone, "What is your destination, Mr. Dore?" I had no idea where I stood, I had no idea if she would let me pass. I replied short and sweet, "Auckland." She asked, "New Zealand?" What was with all the questions? I replied too eagerly, "Certainly is!" She asked, "Are you going for business or pleasure?" I didn't have to think about that one, "Absolutely!"

She stopped doing whatever it was that she was doing. She looked at me, looked like she saw right through me. She knew everything: she heard the voice, she knew my escape plan, it was happening right here, right now. This woman was some kind of psychic, I guess that was why she was in this position. All was over for me. She asked, "Absolutely business or absolutely pleasure?" I stretched my mouth into a big OHHHHHHH, of course! So I said, "Absolutely pleasure, I'm taking a bit of a break from things." She paused again, not a fan of these pauses. I wished she would just be out with it already and let me go or take me away but just stop with the pauses. I did much better when people were upfront with me. She did nothing, did not take her eyes off of me. She paused once again, grabbed a giant oversized stamp and stamped the passport. She folded it up, held it for me and her entire face changed into someone else, she smiled a wide smile, and I took the passport, and she said, "Welcome to the United States of America, enjoy your stay."

I paused to give her some of her own medicine, she did not notice, and I continued on. I made it through, followed the signs to my gate, checked into the gate. Early, I found the lounge, drank more orange juice, ate spicy food - they even had kiwis - and lounged in the lounge chairs.

My flight was called, I approached the gate – I was not so worried this time as I entered through the suction pass between the spaces in the air. I smiled at everyone there was to smile at, and I found my seat – it was bigger than my last seat. I sat down and downed a glass of orange juice. A middle-aged man sat beside me, nodded at me, I identically nodded back. He flipped the footrest up, leaned back in the chair, put a blindfold over his eyes. He was snoring in five seconds flat and ignored the flight attendant's requests to place his seat upright – nobody was getting this guy up. She gave up, and we collectively charged full speed ahead. We were in the air, and I said GOODBYE to Los Angeles. We went up up up and soon over the ocean. They fed me more food, more orange juice, cheese, fruit and I was so full. I started to watch a movie, a bad movie, I didn't remember what happened at the end, asleep by that time.

Woken by my bladder – all that orange juice needed to get out! The man beside me was still snoring, he blocked the aisle, no way around him. I convinced myself I could hold it – who's fooling who now? I wish I had a bedpan or at least one of those rectangular receptacles you put your keys and change in at security. I studied the spaces around the man, looked for places I could squeeze through – maybe under his feet? Finally, I undid my seatbelt – it was time to take drastic action. Stood up, put one hand on his left armrest and one hand on his right armrest, lifted my left leg out in the aisle and propped myself so I was on top of him – wouldn't it be funny if he woke up right about now?

He woke up.

I froze.

He moved his head from side to side. Finally, he stopped moving, snoring again. Five seconds later I wondered what this man was dreaming about, where he came from, where he was going. I wanted to bite his nose – not to hurt him – just a small bite to let him know I was here. My bladder reminded me why I was straddling this man. I slid into the aisle, ran down the aisle, peed the greatest pee ever. I walked back, all the while thinking about how I was going to get back to my seat but when I got there the man was gone. I looked around the plane, I shrugged my shoulders, sat down, looked around the rest of the aircraft but did not see him. Fell asleep.

Woke up to the sound of the alarm on my watch. It was programmed to tell me when I needed to take my medication. I knew enough about myself that this was one thing I could not change. I would like to try without it but there were just so many things changing, and I needed to keep this constant for now. The man was back beside me, sprawled out, I straddled him again

– we were quite intimate for never talking with one another.

In the washroom, I took my medication. Another envelope: PILL #3. This time it actually was a pill – I couldn't think of anything better. I swallowed the pill, it went down hard – always did – you would think I would be used to it by now, but I was not. I hoped my sister had arranged the proper prescriptions with her doctor friend in New Zealand, I did not have an endless supply.

I straddled the man and tried to go back to sleep. The optimal word being tried. Something was going on inside, but different this time – excitement. I felt New Zealand getting closer, and I thought about how it was moving towards me. I thought of it as a person that welcomed me with open arms, and they would say HULLO THERE!

Could not sit still, I took a magazine from the holder, opened it up, there was an article about sheep in New Zealand. In my research, I found out the population of people in the entire country is three million and the population of sheep is thirty million. That means every person could own ten sheep. I read about how scientists are on the verge of creating an inoculation that stopped sheep from farting. The facts said they have multiple stomachs – that's a lot of farts - and the farts accounted for an enormous amount of methane which apparently contributed to global warming. I knew we were very conscious of protecting the environment these days, but those sheep must be full of fear or victory or something if they are farting so much and I thought, Fart away sheep!

I put the magazine down, tried to watch a movie and wondered if they were looking for me back at the hospital yet. Nope, said the voice and I said, Oh, come on, give me some peace already. The voice said, Sorry, and I replied, It's okay just don't do it again. Maybe if I were kind to the voice and didn't put it in a full nelson – perhaps just a half nelson – it would get bored and leave for good.

We were crossing the International Date Line, which meant that all clocks got set back to zero, so I set my watch to zero. This was where time starts and ends and I thought it fitting that I crossed this line. I had already crossed many lines since I left the hospital, but this was an important one because it applied to everyone. It meant that I was included with those that crossed the dateline and we were all the same. I was happy to be among peers as I heard the announcement to fasten your seatbelts, we were landing soon.

The tiny island on the horizon appeared, and it looked like we were approaching slow, but we were going fast. I wanted to jump up and down as the island got bigger and bigger. As soon as we landed the man beside me removed the blindfold – he did not look rested – and we left the plane and I thanked the stewardess.

More customs and for some reason, I was not worried. It paid off, everything went according to plan, I was welcomed to Auckland. I had no bags to claim, I walked into the air – the air was so fresh, it was warm even though it was January. The air, THE AIR smelled different, it smelled like something I had never had up my nostrils before. I asked someone about how to get downtown, and they directed me to a bus. Another bus but a New Zealand bus. We reached downtown, I went to the train station, bought a ticket to Wellington, waited beside the tracks. I listened to people talking, and I liked their accents – some were really thick, I could barely understand them, while others were perfect British-sounding accents. They all seemed like such friendly people, and I wanted to hug them all.

Decided to go for a walk. I had the time, I needed a break. I'd been going for a while and was almost there but not quite. I needed to calm down a bit. I left the train station, and as soon as I stepped on to the road, I could feel his presence. There was a man one block away who approached me. He carried a large bag on his shoulder, had a scratchy beard, unkempt stringy hair, dark circles under his eyes, dirty clothes, dirty skin, black index finger and thumb yellow from cigarettes. He was shouting and the shouting muffled. I wanted to cross the street like everyone else, I wanted to ignore the insanity to join others in looking the other way. I continued walking, I came closer to the man, he shouted, "I know you mother fucker I know you give me money give me all you got so I can get fucked all you rich mother fuckers give me your money I want to bash your fucking brains in I want you to bleed all over the streets!"

Just as we were about to pass we both stopped. He

went quiet, and we looked into each other's eyes. He recognized something in mine, I recognized something in his. I took a breath, and I held the breath inside. His mouth continued to move as he mumbled to himself. He was trying to say something to me – a part of me wanted to listen, a part of me wanted to run, he said calmly, "Give me some money Mother Fucker." I slowly shook my head, not out of pity, out of sadness. A sadness so deep and profound I started crying, tears rolled down my cheeks, I didn't even feel them, and I didn't move. The man took a dirty piece of paper from his pocket, he wiped the tears from my cheeks, he said quietly, "I just want you mother fuckers to bleed all over the streets."

I was still not ready to talk to this man. He was what could always happen to me if I crossed a different kind of line which I had been close to crossing at several times in my life. The only time my sister ever showed a sign of weakness happened when she told me about seeing homeless men in the streets yelling to the sky. She was afraid that could be me, I could slip, and I could fall, and I could be on my own, unable to understand who I was. I tore my eyes from this man standing in front of me, physically moved my head with my hands, took one step down the street, then another, walked away from what I could have been. Walked away from the threat of what could happen to me at any time and it was something I lived with every day, something I fought against every day.

The man had forgotten me already, he yelled at

someone else, "Give me your money mother fucker so I can bash your fucking brains inside out."

My walk was not so successful, maybe it depended on how you thought about it? The station was my best bet at the moment, and I didn't want to miss my train. I sat back on the bench, the train rolled in, I got inside, showed my ticket, kept myself in check. I looked fine from the outside but on the inside, I was screaming, Mother Fucker Mother Fucker give me all your money Mother Fucker I want to bash your brains inside out Mother Fucker.

To take my mind off this, to stop swearing, I glued my face and smashed my nose to the window the entire trip. I saw mountains, lakes, rivers, oceans, more mountains, vast landscapes I had never seen, valleys that went on and on forever. I saw some sheep, I yelled on the inside: Fart away sheep!

In Wellington, I bought a ticket for a ferry, the ferry was leaving in one hour. Walked around Wellington, it was nice, but it was not where I was hanging my hat. The ferry was gigantic, I went right up to the outdoor deck in the back, and I looked down at the motors pushing us along. I thought about the deal they must have had to make with the water. We moved away from the land, but I imagined that the land moved away from us. We were suspended, unmoving, everything moved around us, led us to our destination. When we got far enough away from the land, the engines really kicked in, and we started moving fast.

The other people on the deck moved inside. I stayed

outside alone. The engine was loud. I shouted, yelled, screamed, water sprayed on the deck, and I got soaking wet, but I didn't care. After an hour the engines died down, we approached land from the front, or the land approached us. I was soaked from head to toe. The boat docked. People were looking at me funny but not for the usual reasons, so I didn't care. Besides, there was a lady with a ridiculous mustard yellow hat that looked worse than I did.

I was early for the next train, there was a beach beside the station, I lay on the beach. I took my shirt off, let it and myself dry in the sun, closed my eyes.

Opened my eyes, I had fallen asleep. The train was there waiting for me. I ran for it, put my shirt on while I ran, jumped on the train, sat down, breathing heavily.

My nose was up against the window again as there were more mountains, more sheep, more everything. I was drinking it up – I was drunk. I arrived in Christchurch, there was not much to see. I noticed that there was not much to see in the cities, what there was to see was outside and around the towns, but I guessed people had to live somewhere. I took out my sister's envelope that held Paul Dore's passport and driver's license. Paper-clipped to the license was an address in Christchurch where I was scheduled to pick up the car.

I jumped into a taxi, I said, "Onwards!" The driver didn't appreciate my enthusiasm. He was a small guy, could hardly see over the steering wheel. He looked through the gaps in the steering wheel.

We arrived at the address, the building was an old

mechanic's shop. It was in bad shape. I hung out on the street for a bit to check things out and remembered my sister set this up so nobody should be around to grab me. I rung a bell that was out front, someone yelled, "What?" I yelled back, "I'm here!" There was no response. I heard some rustling, it sounded like a giant wrench or some other tool was dropped to the ground. A large man stepped out from behind a car that was parked inside the garage. He was the largest man I had ever seen, he was a house, and he growled, "Who are you?" He looked mad at me, I must have interrupted something. I said, "Sorry to bother you sir, but I do believe you have a car for me."

He looked at me from head to toe and back up to my head. He looked at my eyes – he knew – and sweat appeared under my arms from nowhere. I told him my sister's name, but he continued to look at me in the same way. He looked me up and down and up and down. His mouth broke into a grin, he said, "Welcome to Christchurch, Paul Dore. My name's Tiny." He had a brand new car for me. Tiny handed me the keys, wished me a nice trip, told me he heard a lot about me from my sister. My sister told me not to ask any questions, so I didn't ask any questions, just thanked Tiny.

I started the car up, it had a beautiful sound, it purred. The only problem was the steering wheel was on the opposite side than I was used to. The steering wheel was on the passenger side, and the passenger sat in the driver's seat. Tiny told me to remember to drive on the left side of the road, and I thanked him for the tip. I pulled on to the road, I was driving on the wrong side of the road already! I put the car on the right side which was the left side. It took a while to get used to it. I drove over a few curbs – I found the left turns especially tricky – there was more car on the left side then you remember. I set out on the highway, I was almost there, just a little more distance to cover.

It felt great to be in a car – I was my own master – I stopped when I wanted, I was not at the mercy of trains or planes or ferries. So that was what I did, I stopped, looked around, I was in no rush, this was the point, I was drinking everything in, I was drunk. I tried to find some stations on the radio, but I could not find anything I was happy with. I turned the radio off, I sang songs I remembered, some songs I could not remember, I made up my own songs.

At one point while driving, the roads zigzagged up and around and down mountains. I was driving and some fog rolled in. It was difficult to see, then I realized that this was not fog, it was clouds. I was driving through clouds. I was driving up up up through the clouds. I wanted to keep driving up into the air past the blueness of the sky and into space. I wanted to park on a star, meet some aliens there and say, "Hello, my friends!" They would welcome me, they would feed me whatever it was they ate, we would live together forever in harmony, and we would laugh at what went on below.

I turned a corner, and there was a car driving towards me in my lane. I freaked out, thought I had finally done it. I forgot, and I was driving on the wrong side of the road. I strangely became calm, continued to drive straight ahead and the other car swerved around – HA, I was right – I was on the right side of the road or the left side, depending on how you want to put it. He was wrong, and I took smug satisfaction in that fact.

Drove clear across the South Island, it was not far. I arrived in the small town of Greymouth. It was called Greymouth because there was a mountain nearby with the same name. It was beside the ocean. I stopped at the ocean, looked out at it, listened to the waves but I was tired, I was having trouble hearing the waves.

The apartment was above a store that sold flowers, maps, other tourist stuff. There was a note on the door, the note was from the landlord, her name was Margaret. The note read: Welcome! I have left the keys under the mat. Looking forward to meeting you! I looked under the mat, and sure enough, there was the key. I slowly put the key into the lock, the key unlocked the lock, I stepped inside, it smelled like wood inside. There was a steep staircase, I walked up the stairs – at every step, my feet got heavier – as I got higher my body felt lower.

I was almost there, my body had been running non-stop, been exposed to stimulations that it hadn't seen in a while and it needed rest. I reached the top of the stairs, the hallway opened up to the small apartment, there were two rooms, it was furnished. The room I was standing in had a small kitchenette, a television, a small couch and a small table with small chairs. I looked in the other room, there was a bed and when I saw the bed

the room started to turn upside down and not even the voice had enough energy to speak. I flopped on the bed.
I made it.
I could sleep now.

Chapter Seven

No dreams. My body and mind were too tired for dreams.

I walked around my new apartment, looked in every corner. In one corner there was a spider, I said, "HELLO!" to my new roommate. The spider was silent, and I was okay with that.

My head filled up with new things: I was here, I made it, now it was time to know what I was doing – why was I here? I understood why, but WHY? All the questions made me pace back and forth.

Out the window was a small balcony, metal stairs led

to ground level. I made a note of this in case I needed to escape.

The pacing made me hungry, I went out for a walk around the town to get my bearings, maybe put things right.

Quietly walked down the stairs, I was not yet prepared to meet Margaret. Another note waited for me on the front of the door. The note read: Hi, I see you got my other note well here's another one to say — Hello and Welcome! What a sweet lady this Margaret. I liked her already, I felt guilty about not wanting to meet her now. Maybe she was still here, perhaps she just stuck this note on my door. Look, an old woman was walking across the street – maybe that was Margaret? I didn't know why but I assumed she was old. I was tempted to stop and talk to this woman, but it might not be her.

Down the street, passed a hostel and a gas station, I found a small diner. Inside, I sat down at a booth like I was a local. The waitress came by with some coffee, her name tag said Sam and she set the coffee down without asking if I wanted it. I did want it, and I said, "Thank you." She replied, "What can I get you?" Eggs, bacon, sausage, toast! It came quick, and I ate fast and in between Sam filled up my cup. Slumped in my seat with a full stomach, I breathed long breathes, felt better. Forgot about jet lag, forgot about how this could affect my system. In the washroom, I popped a pill, skipped the mirror, paid my bill, thanked Sam and was out the door.

I cut between two small buildings. The ocean was

all around me. At the beach, I took my shoes off, my shirt off. The sun was high, and along the beach, the waves kissed my feet. The beach went on forever. I walked forever. I came to a small mountain, the mountain was covered in trees. I found an entrance to a path, inside everything went quiet. Across the path, tree roots crisscrossed across, forcing me to step over them, double dutch style. The air was getting warmer, I wondered where this path led, but at the same time, I didn't care. The earth was getting steep as it turned me towards the sky, the sky shielded by the trees and the leaves, but the sky there nonetheless.

I come to the top after what seemed like a long time.

There was a clearing that led to more beach, the largest beach I had ever seen. I ran down the never-ending path. There was a drop from the landscape down to the beach. As I flew through the air, the decline was more prominent than it looked. Landing on the sand, my feet disappeared beneath the grains.

There was a large tree beside me, it was old, it died a long time ago. The bark was weather-worn, resembled a dinosaur bone. There was no one here, and giant rocks separated this beach from the beach by the town. I padded out to the water, stopped right before where the waves ended. The rocks protruded up out of the water like statues, like someone placed them there, like there was an even larger rock that someone chiseled down from a design in their mind and they worked for years to shape and cultivate what I saw now. There were rocks everywhere: big ones, small ones. There was something about that rock right there. On to the wet sand, water crawled up my feet, kissed my ankles.

There was no one around.

Everyone was gone, I imagined I was the last person, and the gift I received was this beach. I wished I could share this with someone, but I couldn't think of anyone except my sister. I didn't know if she would appreciate this, I think she might, but then I remembered that everyone was gone. The sadness of being alone seeped into me, and someone started talking over my left shoulder. I shook my head, I was alone, I had been alone for so long - did it matter anymore? Companionship was never for me, I tried my damnedest to push anyone of any worth away from me. Sometimes because I had to, sometimes I didn't want to, but it was almost like I never had a choice either way. Being the last person on earth was not so bad, but maybe I didn't know anything else, I didn't know any other way? The voice started whispering again, and I walked to try and lose it. The distraction worked.

Splashing through the water, I looked behind as my footprints disappeared with each wave. I looked forward, thought about the voices, about my sickness, about my mind and how it continually slipped through my fingers. How every time I felt I had grasped it, clutched it, finally held it tight, it dissolved, slipped through the cracks, fell through the spaces between my fingers no matter how tightly I held on.

Without realizing it at first, I started to jog. My footprints become smaller as I ran on the balls of my feet. I ran faster, yelled, screamed. No one was here to hear me. I thought about how my mind was slippery, it always seemed to come and go. Closed myself off from people, closed myself off from myself, disconnected from my heart, cut the wires, built up tall walls around me. The walls needed to come down. The walls were coming down.

My feet ran faster.

I was here to bridge the connection from my heart to my mind once again. Feel the currents running between them again. The energy needed to flow from one to the other and they needed to help each other to make one another stronger.

My feet ran faster.

Let go of what had happened before. I couldn't undo it, I must not undo it, must let go of what was trapped inside that won't leave. Those things stayed in my body, they had slowly taken over, they needed to go but not by force, not by tightening my grasp, they needed to leave by themselves. See them for what they were – files in a faulty system. To fix the system, I must open my hands, open my mind, open my heart and take the walls away, let them go away on their own.

My feet ran faster.

My voice screamed louder.

I had been sick for most of my life. A lot of years to reverse and it couldn't all happen right away on this beach. I knew this, felt this, but I was anxious for it to leave so I could start over. I was sick. I needed to get better. There was a cloud that had been over me for too long. I needed to brush it aside. I would not use force but would yield to the pain, recognize it for what it was worth and see that it was only hurting me. I wanted to remove this, move past this. I had been trapped in my own mind, I had been sick.

My feet ran faster.

My voice screamed louder.

Why was I here? To let go of the pain – never forget the pain but allow it to leave. Here because I wanted to start making choices. A person could change, they could make a choice to get better, not out of force but out of letting go. Here to free myself from me, to fart out all these aspects of my personality and lay them all on the table to see them for what they were. To walk away from what I did not need and keep what I did need. Here to feel the freedom of choice, to pick the pieces of me up and see what it was like to be me, to find out who I actually was, to know that I was a person who was more than his sickness. Here to run along the beach yelling and screaming, not in anger, not in pain, but to release what I did not need.

To let go.

I ran as fast as I could, my legs burned, and the burning felt good – it was a different kind of pain. I hit the wall, another type of wall and collapsed on the sand, the water was cold, the water crawled up around my body. The water told me to relax, the water told me, Everything is okay, you are getting better because you choose to get better. The water was soothing my heavy breathing. I breathed in the thick air and felt something different: I felt free.

Yelling and screaming outside of myself came from farther down the beach. I sat up, saw someone running towards me. The person yelled and screamed like me. I was not the last person on earth, which made me happy. I lay back down to enjoy the final few moments of being that last person on the planet. This other someone got closer. I turned my head towards her, I didn't care that sand was getting in my hair. There was something about that scream, something about that yell, it was full of something I couldn't yet describe. Turned my head back to stare straight up in the sky and wondered if she would run right by me as though I was invisible. My eyes closed. She stopped right beside me, said nothing. Her breathing was loud, and I felt her shadow across my chest. Finally, I opened my eyes, her voice said, "Hello!" Keeping my eyes closed, I said, "Hello." She said, "It looked like fun!" I said with closed eyes, "I didn't think anyone was watching."

This was the wrong thing to say. If it were anyone else, they would have frowned, maybe kicked some sand on me and walked away. She said, "I can't watch anyone having that much fun and not join." And again I still did not get it, maybe I was in a bad mood, maybe I was still jet-lagged, I said, "It wasn't fun at all, it was actually quite painful." Quickly chastised myself for that ridiculous statement as I was actually feeling better than I had in a long time. Who was this person that was talking and why was she still standing here? She said, "You sure know how to have a bad time but look like you're having the best moment of your life."

At this moment, my eyes shot open and I was looking at this woman staring at me. She had the goofiest grin going, bookended by dimples you wanted to push your finger into. Her hair matched the colour of the beach, her skin tanned in a natural way – in a way where someone had been outside a lot because they wanted to. Small nose, slightly flat, remnants of freckles on her cheeks. Her eyes – oh her eyes! Those eyes saw it all, knew me from the inside just from looking. The eyes complimented her hair, and I immediately thought she was a beach and the ocean if the beach and ocean were to take human form.

"Why were you running and yelling?" She asked me. I honestly didn't know what to say, every fibre of every molecule in my body wanted to speak to this woman, wanted to know her, wanted to know what it felt like to walk beside her down the street, wanted to figure out what made her smile and what turned that smile into a laugh. An investigation was needed, and when I found out what made her laugh, I would do that every day.

"People have been asking me that all my life but I never know what to tell them," I said. Maybe that was better. I was just trying to get my bearings, remember where I was and what I was doing here. This person appeared on the beach, on my private beach, on the very first day I was here – what were the chances of that? I started calculating the chances but gave up.

"Come on," she said. She started running down the beach, yelling and screaming. I thought she wanted me to follow. Of course she did, she said, "Come on!" I jumped to my feet, ran faster then I had before and caught up to her, screaming and yelling. We were two wild people running down the beach, yelling and screaming and neither of us cared if someone was watching. Well, I did care if someone was watching, but those usual feelings were getting pushed out of me somehow. Maybe it had to do with the person I was running, screaming and yelling beside on the beach?

She stopped, I stopped. Out of breath, she asked me my name. She did not laugh at the name Paul Dore. She only accepted it for what it was: a name. I asked her for her name, and she said, "Helen." I said, "Get the hell right out of town." She replied, "I can't. I live here." I told her I had met a few Helen's in my lifetime and it was all getting a little coincidental. She shrugged her shoulders.

This Helen in front of me walked up the beach away from the water. A man was sitting on a towel on the beach. He had long flowing locks, his face resembled Helen's face. He had kind eyes and a bit of beard, a tattoo on each forearm. He held out his hand, we shook, his name was Marshall. Helen lay down on the towel, and I sat down next to Marshall. They were brother and sister, owned the hostel I walked by earlier. They heard a new tenant was living above Margaret – it was a small town and news travelled fast. They were happy to meet the new addition, said it was great living here. What we are doing right now was life in this town. No one ever came to this side of the beach, the walk up and down the mountain was too high for most.

Feelings of nervousness settled in. Not from anything Marshall or Helen were doing, but what I was doing. What was going on inside. I stood up, excused myself. They invited me over to the hostel for dinner, I said, "I think I have plans." I had no plans. Excused myself and jumped on top of the dinosaur bone. Climbed up, off the beach, entered the woods, up and down the mountain, back to the town. I didn't remember any part of the walk. I didn't remember what I was thinking. I remembered nothing.

I did not recognize this place where I was. Crossed a street, somehow took keys out of my pocket. There was another note on my front door, guessing it was from Margaret. I ripped it off the door, did not read it. I unlocked the door, stepped inside, slammed the door, up the stairs, inside, I paced back and forth.

Things were supposed to be different. Things were supposed to change. I was supposed to change. Supposed to stop shutting myself out from other people. This was not a big deal to most, but it was a big deal to me. I did not ride on buses, trains, planes to the other side of the world for me to be scared of talking with people. The intention was to establish a different life, one separate from who I was before - a different person with a different name.

Crashing, totally crashing. What was I doing here? This was not right, I was scared, I was alone.

Paced back and forth. At that exact time I said I was alone, the voice chose its moment to come back, told me I was not alone, never alone. It was always there ready to talk if I wanted to. It was sensitive to my needs. It was the only one that understood. The voice vibrated around inside my head, told me what I wanted to hear.

Paced back and forth. Tried to shake off the voice but it told me I had made a terrible decision to come here. I was not trapped before when living in the hospital, I was free, totally free and now I had gone and ruined it all. Nobody wanted to speak to me, waste their time on someone like me, I had nobody, nothing, I was less than nothing, I did not deserve to have an apartment in a town beside oceans and mountains. I had done nothing to deserve this. Give up. The voice told me to give up, pack up, go home before I did something regrettable.

"Like what?" I asked the voice. The voice did not respond, it was not ready to, it knew the game, it was keeping its cards close to its chest, playing them one at a time. The voice went away without responding.

I fell down on the floor, my mind was snapping, the rope got tighter. I grabbed the rug beneath me with my hands tight. The rug was here, the rug was under me, the rug existed. It was in an apartment, in a town called Greymouth, which sat beside the Pacific Ocean on the west side of the South Island of New Zealand. I travelled from far away to get here. I was here, I made it.

I sat up, breathed hard. Long gasps and laboured. Stood up, took all my clothes off, jumped in the shower, scrubbed hard in the shower, tried to get all the sand out of my hair. There were still some grains left. My clothes were getting smelly, I would buy some new ones tomorrow, they should be alright tonight.

Downstairs, another note read, Hello! Sorry, my last two notes missed you! Looking forward to meeting you, Margaret. I felt the warmth of her through the walls.

The hostel was a three-story building. Some people were sitting on the patio smoking. I said, "Hello!" They smiled back, I felt better, I could see better.

Helen sat behind the front desk and when she saw me, smiled a broad smile, her eyes lit up. This made me smile back at her. She called Marshall, who came out and we were all smiling at each other and just stood there smiling. They invited me to the room behind the desk, there was a small hallway that led to their apartment. They had dinner set up with three places. They were expecting me, they told me this and I was smiling stupidly.

Dinner was almost made. Offered me a glass of water, we cheers. This time I was cheersing for someone else besides me. Helen sat down across from me. I almost didn't come, I couldn't believe I almost didn't come, I would have missed all of this. My cheeks hurt from smiling.

Marshall did all the cooking. He was an excellent cook. I was happy to have a home-cooked meal after all the airplane food. We talked mostly friendly-getting-to-know-you talk. It was something I was not used to but was getting easier every minute with these two. Maybe I could do this, maybe I could integrate myself, fit in, disappear? I was comfortable telling them vague details about me, that I was starting over and they respected that. Did not say much about myself, decided I would keep a lid on certain things until the time was right, until I felt I could trust people. Felt I could trust Marshall and Helen, but I still kept the lid on, the lid was unlocked but still closed.

They were orphans, never knew their parents, given up at a young age. They grew up in Christchurch, maybe I walked by that orphanage when I was there? They always stuck together, it was the only way they could make it through. Sometimes it got terrible, but they always had each other. It must be nice to always have someone. They moved here and started working at the hostel. An old couple ran the hostel. The old couple wanted to retire. They gave the business to Helen and Marshall. They had owned it for five years, they were happy.

They told me everything was all cleaned up, but the previous night there was a situation with a guest in one of the rooms. He was about my age, checked in, they had seen him every once in a while. They knew he lived on the other side of the town and some problems existed inside his house that was evident in his eyes. He stayed at the hostel periodically. Helen thought there were times when it was too much to stay at his house. They heard the gunshot early in the morning, went upstairs, found the body slumped across the bed. Helen said she saw his tears. His tears were still fresh, moving slowly down his cheek, the cheek that was not blown apart. It was not the first time she had seen a dead body.

Marshall and Helen wondered out loud why someone would make this decision. This was the point in the night that I was quiet because I knew too many reasons why someone would make that decision. They didn't notice I was quiet. They told me the police came, the room had to be professionally cleaned up. They never saw his father or his mother, people rarely saw them, maybe they went to the hospital?

Changing the subject, I asked about Margaret, and they told me she was the sweetest little old woman. I told them about the notes, they told me she left notes for everyone around town. They asked me what I was going to do for work, I said, "I don't know yet, I am not worried about that yet." We talked more, I felt normal and before we knew it the clock struck two in the morning. I was over my jet lag, and they had to get up early, I thanked them for the food, for their company, they said, "Anytime, how about tomorrow?" I said, "Yes."

On the walk home, there was a halo of happiness surrounding my body in a two-meter radius. The halo was yellow, it sparkled at the corner of my eyes, my feet felt like they were not touching the ground. The note on my door read: Hello! Sorry I missed you again! Would you like to have a cup of tea tomorrow morning? I thought to myself, YES! I walked upstairs, looked around at my tiny apartment, looked around at my new home. I liked my new home. I opened and closed the fridge. Lay down on the bed. Thought about the boy that shot himself in the head. I did not think about why he shot himself in the head, we all had our reasons.

Chapter Eight

Since arriving in New Zealand, I felt good. Better than I had in a very long time. Spending last night with Marshall and Helen was precisely what I needed to assure me that I was acting per my plan. That I was acting normal. That I was being accepted by those around me. That I blended in, disappeared, lived out a life that was quietly reaching out into the sky, grabbing the little piece that was mine.

For many years, I had been on a bed – my muscles went weak, flaccid. Not only was my mind full of instability but my physical body had been separated from my mind. Ignored, cut off, and in addition to bridging the gap between my mind and my heart, I needed to re-establish the connection with my physical body.

Everything needed to work together.

I walked out to the beach, ran along the beach, splashed water in my wake. Jogged at first, but only at first. I pushed myself to run, felt the burn in my lungs, throat, legs. The pain got pushed around my body. I farted it out. The sweat dripped down my face, the sweat trickled down the small of my back. I ran faster, pushed harder, my thoughts drifted along beside me, floated along the top of the water. I suggested to myself that I should keep running, should never stop, just keep going, but reminded myself that I was running to pull myself back together. I was not running from something, I was running towards something. What that something was, I didn't know, but I did know. I didn't want to force it, there were enough forces at work around me. I wanted to work with that energy, bend and manipulate it to put the pieces of me back together again.

I ran back up towards the town. People were walking the streets getting ready for the day. They all stopped what they were doing, all waved to me, smiled. At first, I didn't wave back, didn't return a smile. I thought they were waving and smiling at someone else. It could not be me, but it was me, so I started waving at people before they waved at me. Smiled a giant goofy grin.

Such friendly people here, I wanted to hug them all. I finished my run at the edge of town, I was out of breath, buckets of sweat fell off me, each drop was a part of my old self squeezing through my skin, leaving my body. Drop by drop, I was becoming Paul Dore.

Walking slowly, catching my breath, I came to a house all by itself. This was where it all happened. I realized at once this was the house of the boy who killed himself in the hostel. This was where his family lived. I knew it, sensed it. The house had a strange vibrancy to its energy. The house was old, rundown. There was a long gravel driveway, the lawn was overgrown with weeds that swayed in the light breeze. A rusted truck was parked near the house. The front porch was missing a step. A window on the second floor was broken. The house was painted white or used to be white, now it was a more yellow-rust colour. The roof could cave in at any moment. Random items left around the house on the front lawn: old bicycles, a canoe with holes, flat tires.

It did not resemble a house that people lived in until the door creaked open and out stepped a large man, a man with a long beard and beady eyes. He wore a white tank top, yellow stains under the armpits. He held his ratty pants up with suspenders. He stepped on to the porch, the screen door slammed behind him. He looked right at me. I was staring, I forgot to remember not to stare. I tried something I would not normally do. Usually, I'd run away, but this time I smiled and waved. The man was the first person in the town not to smile nor wave. Thirty awkward seconds went by with me standing at the foot of the gravel driveway and him on the porch. I ran off in the direction I came. I knew that was the boy's father, no mistake about it. I thought about the boy - what kind of life had he lived? I did not think about why he killed himself, I had a good idea about this. I just wondered what he thought about, what he wanted in his life. Did he want more? Did he think there was more? Did he think this was all he could get? The boy killed himself the same night I arrived. I heard nothing, was asleep, a goner. He killed himself that night. There was a significance to that I didn't know yet, so I let it go.

Finished off my run, went home, took a shower. I was meeting Margaret for tea.

The smallest little old lady I ever saw opened the door. Her eyes went wide, she smiled, waved me inside. I introduced myself, she said she knew who I was. I noticed she only had one arm. We sat down, she disappeared, reappeared balancing a tray with her one arm. I stood up to help her, but she waved me off. The tray had a teapot, two teacups. She placed it on the table in front of me, poured the tea.

Margaret's face was wrinkly, she wore glasses that were round circles, her eyes lost among the wrinkles around her eyes. She had a small nose, her hair was slightly coloured purple. This made sense if you were sitting here with her. The apartment was painted purple, all the furniture purple - side tables, lamps, picture frames, her clothes, even the teapot, and teacups were purple. Obviously, she liked purple.

I tried not to stare at her arm or lack thereof, but she caught me, told me she lost it many years ago in an accident. She did not care if I stared, many people did. She got along fine, it happened a long time ago, and she had learned to live without it. Margaret told me she used to run the flower shop, but retired, sold it. She was just taking it easy now, spent her days reading. She worked very hard, never had time to read and was trying to get caught up on a backlog of books. When questions came around to me, I decided to be vague. Marshall and Helen seemed to know when to back off, they could tell when I was uncomfortable about something, but not Margaret. She kept at me until I told her the whole assorted story of my adventure getting here, highlighting the first class lounge, the large seats. I left out the fact that I had taken a new identity, the hospital, that I was basically on the run. The tea was good, but I excused myself, thanked her for the tea. More importantly, I thanked her for the company.

Down the street, I went into a store and bought three new outfits. The outfits were all shirts and shorts, I didn't need anything more than that. At the hostel, I said, "Hello!" to Helen who was working the front desk. I showed her my new clothes, she approved, that made me happy. She asked, "Do you want to hang out with Marshall and me and go somewhere special?" I replied, "Yes!"

At the grocery store, I bought some food, was going to eat properly. Lots of fruit, food that was good for me. Maybe I would catch up on some reading as well. On my couch, I assessed myself so far. Was I doing enough? Was I changing or remaining the same in a different location? The voice snuck up on me, I crushed it back down towards my feet. The voice had not been around today, it did not appear all during dinner last night, did not surface during tea this morning. Maybe it was just hiding out, waiting for its moment to strike? Usually, the voice was always there, never seemed to go away, never seemed to sleep. I worked around it, made it agree with what I was doing. Pleaded, changed its mind, made suggestions to it, made it believe that what I was doing was right.

So happy to be alone. In the hospital, I was so afraid of being alone – it was never a good idea. Lapsed too deep inside myself, hid in my box of criticisms, reviled in them, picked each one up, went over it again and again. I listened to the voice, wanted its approval. I needed to be around people all the time, needed other voices besides the voice, even if those voices were an infomercial on television. The voice was firm, had the creepiest laugh, a wicked laugh, always seemed to laugh when I was at my weakest. The laugh that pushed me over the edge, a laugh of victory.

I lay on the couch, but I could not fall asleep. I had so much energy. In the hospital, I had no energy, and on some days, I could barely move from my bed to the television room. My limbs pulsed with laziness. Now they pulsed with power, pulsed with life. My muscles vibrated.

Good food for dinner, food that fed my new found source of energy. This was a good day, a day where I did indeed what I wanted. There were no blocks, nothing standing in my way. I took things slow, moved my insides around, and everything got nourishment. Instead of being tight as the day went on, I loosened up, thrived here beside the ocean.

Drifting off to sleep, my thoughts were of where I would be going with Helen and Marshall tomorrow. Where would the day lead? Unusual questions swirled around my head instead of the dread of another day that was the same as all the other days. No, now I had high expectations of tomorrow. I looked forward to going to sleep so I could wake up early, instead of sleeping in. I looked forward to what would be offered to me, see what was out there, grab on to what was there. What could I learn from? What could I see to help explain who I was, who this shell of a person had become? Discover for myself the person that dwelled inside the locked down, chained up, boxed in heart of mine.

The next morning I had instructions to meet in front of the hostel at six o'clock. I was early, Marshall and Helen said, "Good morning!" Their small jeep took off, we drove out of the town. The sun rose, the sky clear.

Helen pointed to a mountain in the distance, said that was our destination. I was quiet with excitement. We drove in silence, the talking was accomplished with our eyes. We reached the foot of the mountain, left the jeep in a small parking lot. They each grabbed a small backpack, put on hats that had long flaps to protect their faces and necks. They had an extra one for me, they said I would need it. Also provided me with a pair of sunglasses and we lathered up with lotion as I followed them towards the mountain.

We walked along a path, they told me at the end of this path a staircase began. Long ago, people carved the steps into the side of the mountain. There were over six thousand steps to the top. They asked, "Are you up for it?" I said, "Yes!" They said, "Okay, let's go!"

We reached the end of the path where the stairs began. I looked up towards the top, the stairs made diagonal grey lines all the way up. Some looked steep, some not so steep. Helen and Marshal put one foot on the first step, asked me to join them. They said, "The most important step is the first step." We paused for a second, the wind changed. We started up the steps, we were alone on the mountain, no signs of anyone else. This mountain was put here for us to climb, we climbed in silence, each of us concentrating, focusing, creating a rhythm, a pace that was all our own but somehow we kept in sync.

The voice was nowhere to be found, it had been such an integral part of my life. When it was not here with me, I wondered what plans it was cooking up. On this mountain, I was not as fearful as I once was, I kept climbing.

With each step my mind started to drift off somewhere else, I tried to keep it here with me, but the breeze constantly threatened to pull it outside of myself. Don't fight it, if this was what it wanted to do, let it. Once I stopped fighting the need to clutch on to my mind, a calmness came over me. The movement of stepping up with my left foot, stepping up with my right foot became a moving meditation. My mind felt like it was still attached but floated along with me. I looked up at the top, it did not feel like we were getting closer, it felt in some ways we were getting farther away. This was an old pattern of thinking, and I dismissed these thoughts, not by forcing them, but by allowing myself to recognize, to become aware of the thoughts, let them do what they wanted. To my surprise, my mind drifted back to right now, to what I was doing. It moved down my body, into my legs, into my feet and I felt every muscle working as I climbed the stairs.

Didn't look at the top, just focused on each step as it came.

I recognized the fact that I was getting to the top one step at a time, that every step I took was in the right direction of up up up. I felt a lightness, a sense of understanding. My legs burned, the burning felt good. Every once in a while Helen looked over at me, she smiled, I smiled back. We did not talk, our feet were doing the talking. Halfway, Marshall and Helen asked, "Do you want to stop and rest?" I said, "No, keep going."

The stairs got steep at one point, and the sun was high above us. We climbed on all fours, had gone back in time to when we had yet to stand on our hind legs. I was impressed with the knowledge our bodies held of climbing in this way, as though we had done it before. I felt my body getting tired, my mind full of energy but my body had a limit. We reached the end of a steep set of stairs, I started to slow down.

The voice whispered in my ear. There it was, I had been wondering when it would appear. *You will not make it, you might as well start heading back down.* I pushed the voice away with my gaze, struck it, pushed it down towards the bottom of the mountain to wait for me there.

Helen and Marshall did not notice I stopped. My head had a dizzy feeling, I fell to the ground on my butt with a THUMP. Helen heard the thump, ran back, they surrounded me. I told them I was fine, I was okay. She pulled out a thermos full of water, I took a long gulp. The water tasted good, I felt it run through my body and instantly the dizziness was gone. I stood up, they looked at me, I nodded, they nodded, we continued.

I regained my footing, each step had its own challenge, a challenge that I confronted on my own. Every step represented some aspect of myself that I was trying to overcome, I was mastering it one step at a time. We were getting closer to the top, I focused back down on the steps in front of me.

Six thousand, two hundred and five steps later, we were at the last steep set of stairs. The stairs seemed to disappear into the sky. We could not see the top, I wondered if there were more stairs, the stairs kept moving up, moving towards something that was higher than this mountain. I wondered if, at the end of the stairs, invisible stairs manifested inside our bodies, inside our hearts, stairs where we kept climbing, kept discovering new parts of ourselves. Steps that kept going up, so we never had to come down.

We ran up the last set of stairs on all fours. We reached the top, the air shifted, we jumped up on to the plateau. We made it. We all collapsed on the ground at the top, our bodies had caught up with us, we lay there breathing heavily. Helen's eyes faced my eyes, we looked at each other, we smiled tired smiles.

They stood up, I stay still on the ground for another moment. Something on the ground glittered in the sunlight, and I picked up a small cross-like symbol that must have fallen off someone's necklace. I put it in my pocket for later. We stood and looked around at our mountain, we were surrounded. There were other mountains as far as you could see. We started down a path, the path winded all around, up and down. A person could walk and get lost for hours, for days.

We sat down, ate a lunch that Marshall and Helen had prepared. I felt very taken care of. We still did not talk, we only had stupid grins on our faces. Some clouds moved in, the weather could change quickly up here. We chose a path, walked. We reached a lookout point, I saw the valley, I saw where the earth started to curl around on itself.

There was a heavy mist moving in with the clouds. The mist turned into fog, the fog so thick I could not see Helen or Marshall. Could not see anything, all sound disappeared into the fog, the only sound I heard were small rocks and boulders falling from above on to other rocks below. Everything faded into the fog, my body dissolved, ceased to exist.

My mind drifted along with the fog, moved around, my mind was able to travel to all places all at once. It flew back to the hospital, saw a body that looked like mine, thrashing during the night, fighting with itself, not able to rid itself of the voice that whispered over its left shoulder. The voice told my body to believe in things I had no business in accepting.

My mind drifted along the hospital corridors, saw other patients with their own voices, saw people hurting themselves, saw the nurses playing cards, saw a doctor masturbating in an empty operating room. My mind moved beyond the walls, travelled the same route that I took to get here, felt separate from me, discovering where I was hiding out, threatening to tell others.

I felt the tightness from my dreams, the rope getting tighter. I thrashed about on the bed, tried to remember not to force it, not to help it along in its tightness, but sometimes you could not change things. All connections I had been working towards rebuilding crumbled in an instant.

Instead of feeling grounded, of feeling my feet firmly below me, they were above me. I dissolved in the fog, it threatened to pull me off the mountain, throw me off like the rocks smacking on to other rocks below. I saw my head splitting open. There was no blood, my head popped open like a coconut, two perfect halves.

I scrambled to push around these thoughts to get a grip.

My only chance was to remember where I was, trace

my path. All the steps I took to get here I replayed, everyone and everything. They were all real, I saw them in my mind, reattached the molecules flittering away, caught them before they flew away. I put them back together a piece at a time, just like how we reached the top of the mountain - I took one step at a time, knowing that I was getting closer with each step. The molecules were reattaching, growing, returning me to myself. The voice had not appeared, it did not have to – some things I did on my own.

I felt my feet, felt the rocks below my shoes. Felt my legs, my butt. I let out a fart, felt my insides, my arms, fingers, neck. I reached up with my hands, touched my face, ran them through my hair. I had reattached myself, the fog moved on, the fog let us be. It had taken with it the feelings of dissolving.

The sun returned, I was whole again. Marshall and Helen appeared, they were right beside me the entire time, they saw something in my face, I wondered if they knew they almost lost me, wondered if they cared. Deep breath, pushed the air around inside. We left, headed towards the steps. We had conquered the mountain, took one step at a time back down. I did not look back.

The talking started when we reached the bottom, waiting until we were off the mountain, as though we attempted to maintain a natural balance between us. We did not want to disrupt the energy going up, the assistance from the quiet flow did not want to break any connections by confusing our mouths with our feet.

We sat down on the ground beside the jeep. Helen

and Marshall took their hiking boots off, took their socks off. They did not put any shoes on, and in retrospect, I did not recall them ever having shoes on. They noticed me noticing, Helen said, "We never wear shoes, you should try it." I shrugged my shoulders, said, "Why not?" I took off my shoes, I would not wear any until the day I left this place.

We covered many subjects, we did not talk about the mountain, we talked about who we were as people. They recognized the guard that was up between them and me, and I wondered if I would be able to relieve the guard, wondered if I would be able to ever tell them? As we talked, my mind drifted but stayed present, somehow at the same time. I had known these two people for a short amount of time, but in that space, I had already grown to view them as my first friends. They were here with me, not because they had to be, not because they felt it would help me get better, but because they wanted to be here with me. Maybe saw something in me that was worth having around?

Back in the hospital, and before the hospital, I was alone, disconnected from others. Friends were difficult to come by. The illness did not promote healthy relationship building. I fought with most people, shoved them aside. I did not want them around. Part of it was the voice in my head, the other part was me. It was me that did not want people to see who I really was, what I really was on most days.

Helen and Marshall had quickly become a big piece in the puzzle of me, had already helped to make me feel normal, even though I was growing skeptical of this label. I was not sure what was normal, what was not. There was a little of both inside of everyone.

I always thought that other people were not struggling with their own voices. I watched from my hospital room window and wondered how people on the street were just going about their business, going to work, coming home from work, married, a father, a mother, a brother, a sister? Did they have no problems? Did they have a voice?

There was a shift inside, a change that was making me more at ease with myself. A shift of realizing there were degrees of insanity and fighting going on inside of everyone. Some were just better at hiding it than others. I was never any good at hiding it, that was something I was learning here. Or was I developing a hardened perspective of me? There was a shift going on alright, something on the inside that had been struggling to surface for a while. I lived in fear, a fear so great that I didn't know what to do with it. I listened to the voice, believed what it had said, quenched my thirst on the criticisms it said about me.

I did what it asked.

There was a shift going on, a tectonic shift, one that was moving towards a positive outlook where before I felt afraid, crawled back into bed under the covers, not surface for days. Crouched, moved my body at odd angles, stayed frozen in awkward positions for hours, clenched muscles until they seized, until they lifted me out of bed, forced me to move around. People talked to me, I would not answer, they spoke more and more until I said something.

Then I would come out of it.

Understand that it was something I did not have control over. I told myself over and over that it was coming, that I felt a wave of depression hitting me. It was coming to bowl me over. Every time I thought I could beat it, every time I thought I could compartmentalize it, fold it up neatly, put it into my box for the last time. Every time it came on stronger than before, each time seemed stronger until I was paralyzed, frozen in a shell of a body that could not function. Inside my mind buzzed away, not able to shut down, continually telling me all of the worthless parts of my life, how worthless I was to those around me. Nothing redeemable, nothing resembling a person that once maybe held promise. No wonder I had no friends, I did not want to be with me half the time. The more I thought, the more my mind vibrated, the deeper I got down into that well with the slippery walls, nothing to help me out, nothing but thought after thought of all my failures of a human being.

The idea for this change, this radical change that I knew had to take place in my heart, and my mind came during a dark time. I was out of it for a few weeks. I had gotten the voice under control but depression set in, a deep depression. I wondered if I needed this voice, if it was a part of me that I needed to live, to breath. Was not only in my mind but in my blood?

My body did not stir, only my eyes opened. There

was a weight on my legs. I looked down, my sister was there, she was on her knees, her knees were on the floor, her head was in my lap, her arms were around me. She did not know I was awake, I saw tears forming small puddles on an indentation on the blanket. My sister never cried, never saw tears form in those steady eyes. She mumbled to herself. Was talking to her own voice? Perhaps she hid it well, so I never saw it. I knew this was not the case. I knew it. I knew only that she was sad, that I was all she had, that our parents had gone away in their different ways. We were all we had. I knew that she must have continually lived thinking I was going to go too. How selfish I had been all these years, thinking only of myself, only lived in the expectation that I would get worse. I never thought my sister could be lowered to my level.

Vowed right there I was to get better, I was to be her brother, the brother that she deserved, one that she could be proud of, someone she could introduce to people. My mind started spinning with the possibility that never existed before. One that created a thought, a dim hopeful thought, that I could get better, I could pull myself together. I might never be able to get rid of the voice, but I navigate around it, learn to accept it, to sometimes put it in my pocket.

My sister was not there all the time, she was there for the times that mattered, when I was in my worse states, times where the only hope was in hopelessness. She took a lot of punishment, had to create her own box to put the things inside that she knew were not me.

Confront elements of myself that I could not stand to face alone. When everyone left, when I had nothing else, had no one else, I had her. She talked to me like I was a person, not like I was a patient, not like I was sick. She joked at inappropriate times, she laughed when I could not, cried that one time. I wondered whether she cried not because of what I had become, but she cried for me, cried for me to see her cry so I could see not what I had done to myself, but what I had done to her. I figured I hit bottom, had nowhere to go but up, had been through the worst of it, had lost total control over myself, gave myself over to the voice but somehow regained something. I seemed to have lost everything only to have a thought inserted into my brain that it was not all lost, I could take it back. The feeling was so powerful, I silently cried with her. I felt a surge of power, a surge of energy.

This was the moment the plan started to form in my head.

I reached down, put my hand on her head. She did not move, out of embarrassment or exhaustion. At that moment both of us gave up, we finally gave up. We lay there all night, two fully grown siblings, side-by-side, afraid of what the other was thinking, but hoping it was good, hoping our situations were going to get better.

I got in the backseat of the jeep, we put the top down, drove back to the town. I thanked them for another beautiful day, a day where I opened the portals between the world around me and my mind and I looked inside to see what was there. Liked what I saw so far. I walked down the street in my bare feet. The sun was falling behind me, I waved at others, they smiled back.

There was a note on my door from Margaret, she thanked me for my company. I stepped into my apartment, surveyed my surroundings. I felt stronger every day. I took out the amulet I found on the mountain, felt it in my hands. The amulet was warm, an anchor reminding me of what I accomplished today, a reminder that one step at a time I was getting better, finding who this person was that lived inside of me. The amulet went on the small table beside my bed. I lay down, my mind empty, ready to be filled up tomorrow. My eyes closed, I did not dream.

The next morning, I finished my run along the beach, I did not stop at the house at the edge of town, it was all quiet when I ran by. I scanned the house for signs of life, only the breeze stirred, nothing else moved.

On the beach, I stood out of breath, but less out of breath than yesterday. Removed my shirt, splashed into the water, immersed my entire body. What was underneath me, what swam alongside, what had died below, what part of it floated around me to the top? I held my breath, made my lungs still, floated in the thickness of the sea, disengaged my mind from my body. I allowed it to, chose to break the connection to strengthen it.

Drifting along, trying not to move, I thought about that boy who shot himself in the hostel. What was he thinking before that bullet entered his brain? Before he stopped the flow of thought, cut the wires, broke the connection? Had a voice told him to do it as a voice had suggested to me? Was he alone? I sucked in a reserve of air in my lungs, opened my eyes, my eyes blurry, saw nothing. I allowed them to remain unfocused, feeling the contact between where the water touched my eyes.

That poor boy, someone that had no one, had no choice, nothing. He saw no other option. What was the difference between him and me? What could I see that was deep and dark and inside both of us? Something else lived behind our eyes. I saw a difference, saw a different choice that I had over him.

Once my lungs were void of air, I broke through the surface of the water instead of staying there to fill them up. I burst through the surface of the water, filled my lungs, choked on oxygen, wiped my eyes, my eyes stung from salt. I focused on what was around me, looked at the horizon where the ocean met the sky, and a thought occurred to me to start swimming towards it and never stop.

The thought shook away.

Helen stood on the beach, lightly waving. Emerging from the water towards her, I fell down on the wet sand, out of breath, lightheaded from holding my breath, which I caught in deep gulps. Helen sat down next to me, put her hand on my dripping shoulder. My entire body vibrated from her touch. Helen said, "How was your swim?" I said, "It was good." She said, "I was worried, you were down there for a while." I said, "I was just thinking." She laughed and said, "I can recommend other places with more oxygen where you could think better." I asked, "Can I ask you about something?" She nodded. I asked, "Who was the boy that shot himself in your hostel?" She said, "I did not know him well, nobody really knew him well. His name was Francis Leifhead. He grew up in the town. He was about twenty years old. He was a troubled boy from a troubled family."

When I was twenty, I was gone, so far gone. I was a prophet during that time, I was talking directly to God. He was not talking back. My sister came to see me regularly, she was confused. I grew my hair long, had a beard, always wore a robe and sandals on my feet.

Helen said, "He would stay at the hostel every once in a while. We never charged him for it. He always insisted on paying. We would let him and then sneak the money back into his bag at some point. He was a quiet boy. Polite. He never made a fuss, never complained. He was gracious to stay at the hostel, it was a break for him, that was all he said. After a few days, he would leave in the middle of the night. He would return home to whatever was going on there. Francis was a small boy. His veins were so visible it looked as though he had wires under his skin. He looked unhealthy, needed to eat more. He deserved better. I do not know any more details, it was not good at his house. Everyone knew nobody did anything. I blame everyone, but I really blame myself. In some way, everyone expected something like this to happen."

We walked to the edge of the beach, walked back into town. Helen asked to see my apartment, we went up, there was no note from Margaret. Helen stood in the middle of my apartment, nodded in approval. I was glad she liked it, this was the first time I was entertaining someone. I asked her to sit down, she excused herself, she must return to the hostel, we said goodbye, I was left alone.

Thoughts were pushed away that said there was no point in having friends because they always left. I did not listen, I had listened far too long. I placed it into my box, closed it up, ate breakfast instead.

Went out for a walk, on the surface, I was directionless, inside I knew exactly where I was going. I was slowly working my way to the house at the edge of town, even though I told myself that was not where I was going. As I got closer, I felt the air change, the breeze took a u-turn, spun around, floated towards the opposite direction, pushed me along towards the house until I was standing at the tip of the driveway.

The house was silent.

I heard some creaking, some snapping, banging, like someone continually slammed a screen door shut. I slowly stepped into the field of weeds, the weeds up to my waist. I made a circle around the house, tried to keep the same amount of distance between us. I did not want to get much closer. I continued through the weeds until I saw behind the house the mountain of a man who I met the other day. He was chopping wood, swung a giant axe to a tree stump where a piece of wood split evenly down the middle, the blade of the axe was trapped in the stump, the man wiggled it free. He was not wearing a shirt, only suspenders, the suspenders seemed to be holding his body together. He had extra skin that folded inside of itself only to disappear and come out the other side. His bulges wiggled as he moved a piece of wood on to the stump, clutched the axe with both hands, pointed the axe at the wood, brought the axe over his head, slammed it down, splitting the wood, jiggling his insides. I crouched down in the weeds, did not want him to see me, especially since he held an axe. Maybe he was shy, maybe he disliked people seeing him with no shirt on? I did not want this man to get upset with me. I sat in the tall weeds, watched him thrust the axe down again and again. A pile of wood grew higher by the minute. For a large man, he moved fast, worked efficiently. He exhibited experience and a focus that was lost on people such as me.

Maybe it was being close to a house such as this that emitted some kind of energy, an energy that provoked people into action, propelled them from a calm state of control into chaos. I felt it. I lived in a place such as this before. I understood its pull, understood the inability to get away from it, to always be pulled back until all you could do was push.

I had seen a lot of desperate people in my day, people in the hospital, people out of the hospital. This man fits right in. I studied him, tried to look past those eyes to see what was behind them, to see if there was anything of value, anything I could use, anything I could learn.

I drifted off along the tops of the swaying weeds, my thoughts cracked open, floated across with the wind, disappeared, dissolved, lost the concept of where I was. I did not see the man, could not understand who he was, nor did I care. He did not exist, he was a figment of my imagination, dissolved like my thoughts, disappeared like my sanity. The voice was back, asked why I sat rotting in this field of weeds? I had no answer, started to defend myself, my thoughts broke up.

I lay down on the ground, imagined the weeds growing around me, the weeds snaked into one ear, moved out the other ear, the weeds twisted around my neck, tightened their grip, squeezed. I fought, grasped, could not move them, they only got tighter, thicker, they would not let go. I lost the air from my lungs. It was not like when I was underwater. I chose to push the air out to keep it out. Here I needed it, the air escaped my lungs, every molecule that left my body would not return. I felt the life leaving my heart, felt it ending. I stopped struggling with the weeds, went limp, stopped fighting, yielded.

Immediately, I felt a pressure on my neck, something hit me, pounded against what was constricting me. All went quiet until the next pounding. I forced my eyes open, I was looking at the man with the axe, he chopped at the weed around my neck, pulled the axe over his head, the same focus in his eyes. He chopped down, I closed my eyes, flinched, thought he was aiming for my neck, but he chopped at the weeds, cut through a little more with every swipe. I closed my eyes on the last chop.

I could breathe, move again, I sucked air into my

lungs, snapped my eyes open.

The axe man was gone, the sky dark, the stars out. I stuck my head up through the weeds, I did not know how much I was thrashing about. Was the axe man was real or was he fake? I quickly stood up, did not look to see if someone watched from the house, did not look at the house. I walked in the opposite direction, I did not look up from the road until the breeze had shifted back to normal. I quickly walked home, went a longer way, so I did not have to pass by the hostel. I did not want to wave at anyone, I did not want to smile. I went home, crawled into bed, slept.

Chapter Nine

Time went on, had gotten away from me but in a way that made me happy. Managed to develop a routine, even something resembling a healthy life. I had friends, things to look forward to, also started working a job, and I relished the responsibility.

I woke up in the morning early, went for my run, ran farther every day. I ran towards that something I was trying to find here, that purpose that eluded me so far. I had not found it yet, but I was getting closer with every step, with every morning. After my run, I swam in the ocean, floated along, new memories woke. I was not afraid of them, recognized the memories for what they were, saw them on a television screen in front of my eyes. Laughed, cried, checked my heart, checked to know that my mind was opening up.

Margaret convinced the new owner of her old flower shop to hire me on. Every day after my run, after my swim, I arranged flowers, operated the cash, interacted with customers. Met people from all over the world - they always smiled at me, always liked my flowers. I learned about the process of a flower, the lives of each petal, what they depended on. They needed love, needed care. I was there every day to provide them what they needed, I would not let them down. There were so many different flowers, I learned about each one, learned how to take care of each one, how to create an environment where they flourished. Each one was different; each one was handled on a flower by flower basis.

I had gotten control over my gas problem. I was not farting out of fear or victory anymore. No longer felt afraid. Every day was a victory, every day did not need to be marked by my bowels. I moved my insides around, felt my heart in ways I did not before. I cried in the name of joy just as much as I screamed in sorrow. I did not want to spend so much time alone anymore, I had friends, people that wanted my company as much as I desired theirs.

Helen and I spent all of our time together. We did not touch, we were not ready for that yet, or maybe she sensed I was not prepared for that yet. We had midnight fires on the beach, ate food together, food I never imagined. Climbed more mountains, swam in waters where nobody else swam, talked late into the night.

Helen and Marshall traveled all over the world before settling here. They looked at their orphaned existence as an opportunity to explore, saw a one-way ticket to discovery where others only saw rejection. Helen had a sharp mind for details, I often begged her to tell stories of her travels. She spoke in a voice much older than her looks, she took pity on travellers arriving at her hostel with little money. Helen actually believed in happiness, and for this reason, she was the happiest person I had met. She was making a believer out of me.

Helen had many stories, mostly stories about mistakes, about being in a strange land, not knowing the customs, making it up as she went along. Somehow she survived, through her survival she was stronger for it. Helen filled up my heart, made me feel whole, wanted to know what I thought. She valued what I had to say, always listened, always had an opinion. She was not afraid to get angry, lose control, not afraid to laugh, enjoy herself, feel the vibration of the ground beneath her feet.

Helen often visited me around lunchtime at the flower shop. I gave her a single rose, she placed it in her hair. Sometimes we were silent, but it was never awkward, always comforting. She asked me about my past, I told her about my family, about how my father left, how my mother died in an accident that might not have been an accident. Most of all, I told her about my sister, I told her about how she never gave up on me. I did not tell her about my illness – not yet. I only said I had some troubles, I was here starting over, I was looking for something, did not know what that something was. I told her about the patience of my sister, about the goodness of her soul, that she was still out there working, and I had not spoken to her since I moved here. I missed her. She asked why I didn't call her, I did not have an answer out loud for her. I secretly wanted to be better when my sister saw me, wanted her to be proud of me, to be the person she always thought I was. Soon it was coming, soon I would be ready, soon. I felt it in my heart. Soon.

There was a note on my door inviting me for Christmas dinner in two days, the note said Helen and Marshall would be in attendance. I was not a religious person, not anymore, but I looked forward to tomorrow and the day after.

As I hit the bed, my mind started wondering and assessing how I was doing. I believed I was doing well. I was getting better, the voice was here, always here. I felt in control, it was not getting the better of me. I had gotten into the best shape I had ever been in. Looked forward to the tomorrows in my life like Christmas dinner, like smelling the flowers in my shop, like running, like swimming.

The next day I walked over to the hostel, sat on a bench across the street, watched the entrance. I saw

Marshall working at the front desk. No Helen. Sat waiting for an hour. In the hostel lobby, Marshall was filling out some forms. He looked up, smiled at me, walked around the desk, hugged me. I wanted to stay in that hug longer, but he pulled away. He asked, "What can I do for you?" I asked him if I could have a room, he thought I was joking, I was not. I asked him, "Can I have the room that Francis Leifhead stayed in?" He told me, "We haven't rented it out since the accident." I liked Marshall but calling it an accident bugged the hell out of me. I insisted, he shrugged his shoulders, said okay. He started writing my name on the ledger, I asked him if I could have it unofficially. He thought about this, nodded his head, gave me a key, said, "Helen will be happy to see you." I only nodded my head, flashed him a smile. It was a phoney smile.

Standing on the landing of the second floor, I looked at the key to double check the room number. Found the door, put the key in the lock, unlocked the door. Air came out of the keyhole like the room sighed. Pushed the door open, the light from the hallway illuminated a rectangular line of yellow into the room. Inside, I closed the door behind me. Stood in the dark, I felt a presence, like someone was here with me. It was not the voice over my shoulder, this was something else. I flipped the light switch expecting someone to be sitting on the bed looking at me. I was alone in the room. Dropped my bag on the floor, opened the window. A gust of wind swirled into the room. I sat on the bed, inspected the room. The small bed was against the wall on one side.

A wooden chair, a small side table beside the chair, a closet with a mirror on the door.

A picture hung on the wall over the table. The picture was of a man running along a beach. The sand yellow, the ocean bluer than in real life. The man had a determined look on his face. The room must have been cleaned up after the 'accident'. The bed was made. A shirt hung in the closet. I wondered if this was Francis Leifhead's shirt? I took it off the hanger, smelt it. Musty. I took off my shirt, put his on. Under the bed, there was nothing but cobwebs in the corners. I turned off the light, lay down on the bed. The presence came back in the dark. It lay down beside me. I asked it what it was, but for now, it was silent. I thought back to the first time I was in Greymouth. Pictured it in my mind, tried to remember if I was in this room before and if there was something familiar. I could not find anything. I wanted to fall asleep, but there was a pressure in the room around me that grew with the darkness. It pressed against my body, kept me alert, kept me wondering, what happened? Who was Francis Leifhead? Was he someone that I knew? Maybe someone that needed my help? A call from the darkness that I ignored? Was I not ready to hear again? Perhaps I was scared to step into that darkness again? Maybe this time I would not be able to get out of it? I finally drifted off, dreamt of the tightness, the rope around my neck. I could not see who the people were that pulled on either side of the rope. They were careful not to show themselves. Woke up sweating, short of breath. In the morning, the room looked different.

At the top of the stairs, I waited until the front lobby was empty. Walked out into the fresh air, the first thing I wanted to do was go to the Greymouth newspaper office. It was a small paper that focused on local stories, run by an elderly gentleman named Tony. He moved slow, but he got the paper out once a week. He wrote all the stories, took all the photographs, delivered to everyone. The office door opened with a chime. Tony looked up from his desk, I introduced myself, he said, "I know who you are. Greymouth is not that big." I asked, "Can I see the issues that included any reference to Francis Leifhead or his family?" Tony got the papers, had them all organized by date and by year. He handed them to me, shook his head, said, "Damn shame what happened to that kid." I nodded my head, sat down at a reading desk he provided for residents.

Francis Leifhead. There were two articles about a small legal battle between the town and his father over his land. There was a photograph of his father, it was the man I saw outside the house when I was there. He looked just as menacing in black and white. The article did not say much, only mentioned his two sons Francis and older Xavier. The other article was about Xavier. He left Greymouth, worked as a stuntman on some movies that were shot in the city. Then there were the articles about Francis, about the accident. Again not much information, only facts. Hinted at vague troubles at home, discussions about where he might have gotten the gun, possibilities of why he did this. The articles provided no answers to the questions I had. I did not think this was going to be easy, but I thought it was going to be easier. I handed the papers back to Tony, thanked him, asked him about Francis. He shook his head, said, "Not many people know what went on in that house. They kept to themselves, were not really a part of the community. I have my guesses just like everyone else." I asked him, "What are your guesses?" He only said, "The kid had a rough life. That father of his was a tough guy. Rumour was he had a bad temper. Worked in forestry for many years until he had an accident. Been living off disability assistance. Never leaves the house, grows his own food in a garden. Anything he needs, he has it delivered."

Over at the grocery store, I asked for the owner, Greta, if there were any jobs, she said, "It is your lucky day, I need help part time around the store cleaning up and to make the odd delivery. Can you start tomorrow?" Over at the flower shop, asked if I could work part-time for a few weeks. The flowers helped calm me. I liked learning about them. I spent some time with the flowers, I needed some strength. Remembered that to find out the truth, I needed to gather strength. Needed to be strong and think clearly. I was still working at keeping the connection between my heart and my mind. It was difficult. I continually became distracted, why this was so hard?

Forced myself to go for a run, ran along the beach. My beach. The one where I discovered so much. It felt different. My mind was not here. Swam in the ocean, tasted the salt in my mouth. The salt tasted different.

Continued running. Ran out to Francis Leifhead's house. The long grass was still there, nothing had changed since the last time. Nothing had changed since the photograph in the newspaper article. It looked deserted, but I knew he was in there. I wondered if he watched out the window, looking at me, had been waiting for me to return? Maybe he had no idea who I was? Did not care who I was?

Back to the hostel, stayed across the street between two buildings. Made sure Helen was not around. The coast was clear, I quickly scurried up the stairs into the room. I stood in the darkness of the room, the presence was still here. Felt a little different, it was changing. Maybe it knew what I had been doing? If it approved? Perhaps it just wanted to be left alone? Perhaps it was just a figment of my imagination? Maybe I would forever look for things in the darkness until I become a part of it?

I lay down on the bed, the presence snuggled next to me. It scared me because it was a different kind of darkness, one I felt comfortable with, one that welcomed me into its arms. A comfort that I could get lost in. The darkness I'd been used to for most of my life, darkness that fought with me, drew me into constant conflict with myself, threatened to rip apart the connection between my mind and my heart. My next step? I did not know. What was I doing? Why could I not just drop all this? Move on, move forward with my life? Put these things in a box, shipped that box away. The other side said that if I did not deal with this, it would come back in different ways, manifest itself throughout my life, never leave me alone. Even if it destroyed me, I had to find the truth.

There was a shadow over me. I felt it on my body. I opened my eyes expecting Francis Leifhead telling me to leave him alone, to take his shirt off, stop bothering his father. Instead, Helen stood over me, watched me, did not say anything even when she saw my eyes open. She just sighed, sat down on the chair. I sat up, we faced each other in the small room. We did not say anything for a long time, I did not know what to say.

And then something happened, feelings I had been keeping from myself welled up, thoughts that I shoved way down into one of my boxes flooded my insides, and I could not contain it anymore. There was just something about a real live person sitting here who wanted to be around me, who worried about me, wanted to get to know me better not because of anything else except for who I was.

I exploded with words, there were tears in my eyes, sometimes I saw tears in her eyes. I told her everything. It went like this: My parents forgot about my sister and me, my father was an asshole and left, the burden of his family was too much, I still did not understand why we were too much or why he decided he had to, but he did. My mother killed herself in an accident, it was considered an accident, but my sister and I knew better, my sister thought she killed herself in this way so we could have the small insurance claim on her life.

I thought she died of a broken heart, not because my father left us, her heart was broken thinking about another life, the one she was supposed to have. I had contented myself with believing she died with a smile on her face, that she was rid of us all. After that, it was only my sister and me. She quit school, started working. She did not need school, she was a smart person, she got suntanned standing in front of industrial-sized pizza ovens. She knew she would not be there forever. I had already started acting strange, the illness that has plagued me my entire life, that probably began in my mother's womb took shape, it still troubled me to that day, as I sat in that room with Helen. It led to me being hospitalized for three years after I tried to commit suicide. I saw things that I now know were not there. Heard people who talked in my voice, other people that were not me. I carried with me here a voice, the one that was with me first. I was hoping it would leave me be, not find any reason to bother me here.

"Then there was Francis Leifhead," I said. "He killed himself the same night I arrived here. I had to find out what happened, to find out if I had something to do with it. I left the hospital, travelled here with the help of my sister. Like I said, she was a smart person, she got involved with some people, let's just say she was a business person of sorts. I wanted to start over, I thought I was better, wanted so much to get better. Felt settled here, like a new person, like it might be possible. I met you and Marshall, you made me feel like a whole person. I got a job, a place to live, but there was an itch, something not yet worked out I had to see. It was worse than I thought, it only created more questions, fewer answers. Now here I am in the environment of my new life telling you, the only person besides my sister, who has reached out, shown me that they cared about me, that they wanted to get closer to me. This was hard because sometimes I did not know who I was and I get scared that you will get closer to a person that you might not like. You would reject me. We would both move on, and I would continue to move through the world unsure of where I belonged, if I belonged anywhere when all I wanted was to be rid of these thoughts, send the boxes away. I want to belong here with you."

I collapsed on the bed, exhausted from all the worries, all the thoughts that would not stop buzzing around in my head. My body ached, physically hurt to release all these things that never seemed to have enough room, that never left, only festered, grew. I just could not take it anymore, my body went numb, I felt nothing below my neck.

I expected Helen to cast me away, to be horrified by what I said. I had never said all this to one person all at once. For lack of a better word, it sounded absolutely crazy. None of it made sense, not even to me and it was my life. Helen said not a word, did something no one else had ever done. She pushed me over, lay on the bed beside me, put her arms around me, held me close to her. She lightly kissed me on the forehead, gently rocked me back and forth.

Feelings in my body come flooding back. I felt every

molecule on my body, the molecules all ached, but they ached for her. Wished I could die right now and come back new and improved. No one in my life ever held me. My sister hugged me, but she was not the most affectionate person. I knew that when she did hug me, it meant something, it meant I was supposed to remember it. I did remember every hug she gave me. I received more strength from those hugs than all the trees, lakes, mountains – the hugs kept me going.

This was something else entirely.

Helen's touch was not one out of pity, it was warm. It was putting our bodies in parallel, drawing strength from each other. There was something I could only refer to as love resonating off her body. The love enveloped mine, we intertwined our legs, I put my arms around her. The tears came, it was a rainstorm. The tears poured down my cheeks, the tears were different than ever before. Weeping, I hardly breathed. Tears flooded the bed beneath us, they were tears of happiness. Happiness that I was here with her. They were also tears of absolute sadness that I was teetering on the edge of regressing back to my old self. They were tears telling me this was where I belonged, in the arms of this great woman. I cried because she listened to me, heard my story, and she did not care, had no commentary, no ideas on how I could get better, she just listened and accepted that I was ill, that I had problems. Maybe she had problems she had not told me about? This was what I learned travelling all around the world, was that everyone had problems, everyone dealt with them in different ways. Maybe if we all just admitted that we were all a little crazy, that our hearts and our minds were disconnected, we could do something about it, we could fix the damage, restart the machines within each of us that had been broken. Only once I fixed myself, once I reconnected to myself, then I could reconnect to living, breathing people and leave the voices, the insecurities, the feelings of inferiority behind, move forward into a life that I deserved to be living.

Helen cried with me. We wept for each other, for the world. We stayed in bed all day. We finally stopped crying when the sun went down. She peeled herself off of me, left the room without saying a word. She had said enough, more than enough. The door shut, the darkness settled in around me. I felt emptied out, the tears had dried on my face, the sheet was still damp with tears. The tears had made shapes that represented different times in my life I was crying. I could not move, did not want to move. I drifted off, something had been carved out of my mind, it was clear for the moment.

I rushed to the grocery store the next day, apologized to Greta for being late, told her I was sick, asked her if I had lost my job, she said, "Of course not, just get to it and can you make a delivery out to the Leifhead house?" The air went out of my lungs. She gave me the list, told me instructions, said to leave the bag on the front porch. There would be an envelope with money. Take the envelope, leave, do not ring the bell, do not knock on the door. I collected the items on the list from around the store.

The air changed the closer I got to the house. I thought that maybe these changes in air pressure were figments of my imagination. I tried not to think about that for the moment. Along the road, the grass grew longer. I paused at the end of the long gravel driveway. The house looked the same. My head was clear from last night, there was more room for thoughts to bounce around. I felt my thoughts ping-ponging against the side of my skull. Took in a breath of fresh air, held it for as long as I could, let it out. At the same time, a fart escaped my backside.

I stepped off the road towards the house, climbed into some kind of vortex where the air was thicker, harder to breathe, harder to walk, like I was underwater. The long dead grass swayed on either side of the driveway. I felt like the grass was trying to tell me something but I heard nothing. I reached the house faster than I thought, sooner then I hoped, wondered where this sense of fear was coming from after all of the things that have happened to me.

At the steps leading on to the porch, I inspected the house, tried to look in the windows. Nothing. The house was old. One of the front windows broken, the railing running along the stairs rotting. On the first step, I heard a voice. It startled me. I had quickly gotten used to hearing only one voice. Took my foot from off the step, the voice went silent. I stepped back on the step, the voice returned. I couldn't make out what it said, the voice only mumbled. It was a young sounding voice, it was not telling me to do anything, it was just there. I stepped on the second step, another mumbling voice appeared, it sounded older than the first one. The voices were talking to each other, they talked about me for some reason, they calmed my fear. I did not feel they were here to hurt me, they were just here. Maybe I was better off, even happy that someone was here, someone besides the man that lived in this house.

I stood on the porch, the inside of the house was still, it had the feeling of someone trying to be quiet, trying not to be noticed. I put the bag of groceries beside the front door. There was the envelope resting between the screen door and the frame. I put my hand on the handle, sucked in air, held it there, put my other hand on the envelope. I opened the door, let the envelope fall into my hand.

There was an influx of air.

The front door was pushed open an inch by the breeze.

Creaked.

If the silence could speak, it said, "Quiet!" I held the screen door still. Pushed out the air in my lungs. Moved the front door open another inch. The door did not creak as much. Looked through the crack in the door, saw a front hallway that led towards a dark room. Turned my head, there was a doorway into a hall. I saw a living area, the arm of a couch. Something struck me right away - the house seemed empty. It also looked incredibly clean on the inside like it had been taken care of, while the outside had fallen into complete neglect. I imagined that the owner wanted to create an image to his neighbours, presenting an individual that was unkempt, dirty, unreliable, when all the while on the inside he was immaculately disciplined in the art of cleanliness. I pushed the door open another inch, saw something in the darkness at the end of the hallway. I leaned in closer, it hit me, the door slammed shut, the voices pulled my head out of the doorway. I stumbled backward, fell on my ass, the bolt in the door fell into place, it was not the wind that slammed the door, it was not the wind that twisted the bolt, it was Leifhead. He was standing on the other side of the door when I peeked into his house. He was standing on the other side of the door right now. Frozen, I stared at the door. There was an eye looking out the peephole. It stared at me, I stared right back. I stood up slowly, never taking my eyes off his eyes. Neither one of us blinked. I was in some kind of standoff, I let him win this game, picked up the envelope, turned to step off the porch.

A voice came from inside, the voice said, "What are you looking for?" I stopped mid-step, almost fell off the porch. Spun around, where was all this courage coming from? I said, "I was looking for you." What the hell did that mean? I knew it was the truth, but what did I hope this would accomplish? The voice replied, "Looking for who?" I was not getting anywhere fast, I answered, "Who do you think I was looking for?" There was silence on the other side of the door. I did not want any more questions from this man, I wanted answers, I said, "I want to know what happened to your son, Francis Leifhead." The voice answered quickly this time, "My son is dead. Shot himself like a coward." There was a change in his tone during this answer, there was something more. Maybe I was on to something, I said, "I think there might be more to it than that." The voices tried to pull me away, they knew something I did not know. They were ahead of the action but not quite far enough forward.

The door was thrust open, the big man I saw a long time ago with suspenders, a large belly, and scraggly beard, engulfed the doorway. He was fast for a man of his girth. He lunged at me, grabbed me, threw me against the wall of the house. Picked me up again, hurled me through the screen door. I broke the screen, landed in the hallway of the house. I was stunned but not stunned enough to realize I was inside. Leifhead headed towards me, ripped the remaining screen from the door. I looked behind me at the darkness, I needed to know what it was that I saw at the end of the hallway. I picked up my aching bones, ran down the hall, slid along the wood floor that looked like it was polished this morning, reached the end of the hallway, dived headfirst into the darkness. A solid object that I could only decipher was Leifhead's fist thumped me at the base of my neck. I crashed to the floor, blacked out. Before I blacked out, I saw a shape in the darkness that had rounded edges, in the middle of the shape was a light, the same light I saw at the bottom of the lake long ago. A light I had not seen since. A light that I had been chasing for too long. The first time I saw that light, I almost drowned. Before I blacked out, I wondered if I was going to die for real this time.

I came to, the back of my neck ached, my body ached, I opened my eyes, I was laying in the tall grass, the sun setting. The envelope with the money was taped to my chest. I sat up, I was at the edge of the driveway near the road. Stood up, regarded the house from a different perspective, something was pushing me away.

Walking on down the road in a daze, I reached the grocery store, gave the envelope to Greta, she asked what had I been doing all day. She got a better look at me, commented on my sad look. I told her I was speaking to Mr. Leifhead, she said to me I was not to talk to him. I asked her if I could go home, I needed to lay down, I was not feeling well.

Arrived at the hostel, crossed the foyer, Marshall was standing behind the desk. I did not even see him. Upstairs, I fell on to the bed. Thought about the light, wondered what happened. Did I cross over into a different world at the end of that hallway? Why did he leave me laying at the edge of the road like garbage waiting to be picked up? Did he want to kill me? What was he hiding? Did I have something to do with all this? Did he know who I was? What about Francis? Who were those voices talking to me, trying to warn me? My head buzzed, there was too much information, I could not sort through it, put it into the proper boxes, so I just held it all inside. I felt delirious, thrashed around on the bed, fell on the floor, curled up on the floor. I watched the spider under the bed building his web. I wished I could be that spider, not a care in the world except the building of his web, the catching of some flies.

At some point, someone came into the room. Helen, I hoped it was Helen. The person helped me into the bed, cleaned me off, put ice on the back of my neck. The ice was cold, I felt it all the way to my feet. I talked out loud, wondered about the voices, the ones that were in my head. These new voices were trapped to the confines of the lemongrass, the house that was falling apart on the outside, so clean on the inside you could eat off the floor. I thought about my own voice that vibrated in my head, fluttered around. I felt it was on my side, but as I drifted off into a restless sleep, I wondered if this was only a new voice, one created to finally end my days, to get me on its side just to take everything away all at once. The person who I hoped was Helen left, I was alone but not alone. My head swirled around, thoughts bumped into each other. I would never find peace. At least the last thought in my head was of peace, even if that thought said I would never find it.

I went to the flower shop in pain, my neck hung at an unusual angle. There was only one position I could hold it where it did not hurt. I wanted to be with my flowers, to try and help me sort through this information, to discard what I did not need. This had become difficult. Something told me I needed everything if I was to figure out what this all meant.

This was stupid.

I had nothing to do with Francis Leifhead shooting himself. I needed to stop, needed to find peace. How could I find peace when I did not know what it was? Maybe I could be at peace knowing that I might have found something at some point in my life – would I see it again, only to drift off, get the wild eyes, scare homeless men, shout in bars?

I got into bed, and darkness crept into my mind. Anger took over, directed my actions, made moves without asking. I was embarrassed with myself. I wanted to crawl into a ball, hibernate until peace came, whenever that would be. What was I doing here? My mind searched for answers, searched for the details, none came. I tried to cry, no tears came. I wished Helen visited me. Why could I not go visit her? Nothing was opening up for me anymore, everything was shutting down, closing up. I felt I was getting to a point where something had to give. I was scared that it might go a different way, back into the darkness, into a place I had fought so hard to stay out of. I could not help it, I needed to turn on the lights, needed to find what the definition of peace was so I knew what it was when I saw it.

The running, the swimming used to be a source of revelations. Now they were constraining. I only thought of Francis Leifhead during the runs and the swims. What was it like living in a house with that man as a father? I just could not help but think there was something more to it than simple physical things. I still needed to find out more, find out anything that swept away the cobwebs. What happened during the lost few hours before he died, before he presumably shot himself? Why didn't I think of this earlier? The police.

Finished my swim, got out of the water, walked all around the town, found nothing that resembled a police station. Tony in the news office told me the nearest police station was in the next township. The policeman that handled the case should be there. I jumped in my car, found the police station a half hour away.

The views were spectacular, I hardly noticed them.

Parked beside the only police cruiser. Dust settled on my car, spread like larvae on to the police car. I let the engine relax, relaxed my breathing with it. Closed my eyes, tried to hear my breath, tried to feel that connection from my heart to my mind. Faint, but it was there. The police station was small, simple. A desk with filing cabinets, behind the desk a chair on either side. Even a tiny cell with bars going from the floor to the ceiling.

The police officer looked up from his paperwork, smiled a smile of a man that had a job where nothing much happened. The crime rate of the surrounding areas mainly consisted of people fighting over land, maybe having one too many pints at the bar and getting into it with their best friend. After talking with him for a few minutes, the most violent thing that the officer ever saw so far on this job was the suicide of Francis Leifhead. When I mentioned the boy's name, some kind of strange shadow covered the officer's eyes as he looked towards his desk. For some reason, the wind picked up at that point. The officer asked who I was, what I wanted with the information, the standard procedure. I told him I was new to Greymouth, that I had a run-in with the boy's father, heard what had happened, was interested in learning more. The officer was difficult to convince, reluctant to provide me with anything, but he perked up when I mentioned the Leifhead father. He told me he never even got a chance to talk with the father, he seemed to have disappeared. They even had him as a suspect at the beginning, but then it was clearly a suicide. I told the officer that he looked like a movie star in one of those old classic American outlaw movies. He smiled, shuffled into his filing cabinet, pulled out the file on Francis Leifhead.

The only other place to sit was inside the cell. I went through every inch, every piece of paper in the file. Committed it to memory. There was a breakdown of the events leading up to Francis Leifhead pulling the trigger. Photographs, witness accounts. One of the witnesses was Helen, another one Marshall. They were articulate and actually sounded shocked. There were ballistic reports on the gun used, the bullet that shot through his head. I took it all in, memorized everything. Closed my eyes, tested myself on the information. I was there for the rest of the day – for hours. I was there until the officer kicked me out. I handed the file back to him, thanked him for his help.

I drove fast but not too fast back to Greymouth. Stopped beside a small lake, sat under the tree with some pens and notebooks that I brought with me. Went through every piece of information I read today, that I memorized sitting in that cell, filling up my In

Box. Now putting it in the Outbox and down on paper.

Wrote down reports about Francis, recited to myself a psychiatric assessment that was put together after his death. There were many holes in the report, many grey areas, should of's, could of's, might've beens. Some of what was in the report constituted complete lies, I could tell, but I was not here to judge. I sat by this lake, wrote down information and more information. The day turned into night, I wrote by the lamp in the car, shut off my mind while I wrote. Took breaks, sometimes I stepped out of the car, stood by the lake, beside the tree. I did not think I even saw the lake or felt the strength coming from the tree. Only wanted to write, unload the information. The only time I stopped writing was to read the witness report by Helen. It was a paraphrased written report of her interview. I read through it carefully, looked for Helen's voice as much as anything new on Francis. Her report on the incident was fully representative of Helen. I heard her singing it over my left shoulder. She talked about what a sweet boy Francis seemed to be, that she did not know him well, that he was quite isolated out there on that farm, but she saw him walking around town every so often. The one thing she remembered was he always smiled at you. When he looked up, he seemed to look right into your eyes, right into your thoughts and he smiled. He would not be trying to hide anything or to pretend he could not see less than he could. Helen remembered the boy checking into the hostel and how he barely said a word. Again, she felt his eyes on her, there was a story coming from him that he was not telling her, she did not think much of it. Everyone knew about the Leifheads, they seemed to be the family that existed in all communities. The family that might have had some secrets, where some things might be going on that others would not approve of, but who isolated themselves from the town, from other people for a reason. No one felt compelled to visit the farm or get to know the boy or his family better.

Helen told the officer that we were all complicit in Francis taking his own life, that we ignored him, passed him in the streets all knowing what was happening on that farm or at least knowing that something was happening. None of us stopped, none of us asked the boy how he was and if he needed any help. His eyes seemed very kind, he probably would have refused any help or just said he was fine.

I was struck with Helen's insistence that everyone around Francis might have also pulled the trigger. This threw me off, made me wonder if I had been all wrong about this. I also noticed that Helen was the first person who referred to Francis as killing himself, all other references to him mostly said The Accident or The Incident.

I finished writing my notes, the inside of my car filled with paper, threatened to spill out of the windows. I tried to make order of it, tried to make sense of it. Neatly organized the pieces of note paper, putting appropriate information into a timeline that created the story that happened that night or at least the timeline that the police gathered data on. I wondered where I fit into all this? There was no sign of me, I could have still slipped in and out somehow, I could not recall a few hours. From looking at this information, there was still a time period that was not accounted for. Nothing explained what happened during those hours. I had all the papers, the contents of my mind had been spilled, the Outbox was empty. I looked around at the pieces of paper, thought about how the contents of my mind filled up the inside of a car, wondered if I calculated every thought I ever had, what would that fill up?

I opened the door of the car, stood by the tree, by the lake. Remembered all the strength I had gotten from the trees. Touched the tree, felt nothing. I wondered if I was losing all connections between my heart, my mind, my body, the trees, the water, the mountains. When would I be able to gather my strength from these things that have provided me with so much more in the past? I took my arm off the tree, stepped away from the tree. Sat down by the water, dipped my feet in the water. Cold. Kept my feet dangling in the water, stared across the surface of the lake to the other side where the sea met the land. Slowly I started moving around my insides, things started shifting. I only saw the water, the tiny waves being made by the breeze blowing. My eyes fixed on the exact point in front of me where the water met the land. It seemed to speak to me, it was trying to say something to me. I could not make out what it was, felt a pressure, lost track of everything, I no longer saw the trees, the land, the water. I only saw the faint line that stretched across where the water met the land. Water was dangerous. Found out when my gaze shifted, the line where the water reached the land shifted all on its own, the wind changed direction, the waves fell over each other in different ways. It changed my perspective, fooled with my physical body. Leaning my weight on the earth, it left from under me, I fell into the water, the water was cold, shocked my body. There was no white light in this lake, only darkness, thickness. I cut through the surface, looked towards the horizon, crawled out shivering. Leaned against the tree, the tree was not warm, the tree was not comforting.

Something opened up inside, the cold had taken possession of my ability to create distractions. All I saw was where I was right now, where I was going, why I was doing this, and I could not answer. Yes, there were a few hours unaccounted for, but how could I have possibly been responsible for this? I must be wrong, but every shiver from the cold added weight to the feeling that I pulled the trigger, allowed the flow of that bullet to shatter that boy's head.

Somewhere in all this, I fell asleep only to wake up shivering more than before. Picked myself up, headed over to the car, opened the door, pushed some papers off the driver's seat. The vehicle moved under my weight, started the engine, drove down the road, somehow I made it to Greymouth.

The hostel was not an option. I just could not do it tonight. Found a note on my front door from Margaret, I did not read it. Headed upstairs, the apartment the same as when I left it. Took my clothes off, fell on the bed, crawled under the covers. So cold, so fundamentally cold right down to the bones. At least the cold had shifted my thoughts away from the usual.

Woke with the sun shining on my body, into my eyes. Felt different today, lighter. Got up, decided to go for my run. Ran past the Leifhead house, saw no signs of the big man. I was not scared, I just did not care. The white light popped into my head, something I was not prepared to see. The white light opened up, shone at me wherever and whenever the time was right. I knew it was in that house, I knew it. I should not sneak around through the yellow grass into the backyard, but of course, this was precisely what I did. There was a porch that was falling onto the ground, it creaked when I stood on it. I looked in the window, the window covered except for a small slit in the corner. Tried to make out something, anything. There was no movement, in the corner lay a pile of wood. I picked a nice solid two-by-four that with a thump I should be able to take down the big man if he tried to tackle me again. Opened the screen door, it fell off the hinges in my hand. Almost dropped it. Leaned it against the wall, turned the doorknob, pushed inwards. I got my two-by-four ready, opened the door, paused. No one slammed the door shut. I opened it an inch at a time until I could slip through the door. Stepped inside with one foot, the other foot joined it, my body snuck inside with the two-by-four by my side. The house was as clean as ever. No sound, nothing. I was in the room where the white light appeared. There was no sign of it. Stepped into the hallway, came to the living area.

The big man sat on the couch, he was missing his head.

There was a shotgun that had fallen to the floor beside him. His body leaned over the arm of the couch in an unnatural posture. I felt sick, my knees shook, I looked away, but I saw a note. There was a note that had fallen to the floor, there were specks of blood on the piece of paper. Took a breath, tried to fill my lungs but coughed, closed my eyes, did not want to see this, but I needed to know what it said on that note. Tried to convince myself I was not responsible for this, all my hours were accounted for, he inflicted this on himself. I opened my eyes, inched over to the body, stepped in between the drops of blood. Reached down for the note, made the mistake of looking at the headless body, the pieces of brain, skin, tissue all reformed the big man's head.

It all happened so fast.

He started screaming, spoke in the same voice as the one that used to be over my shoulder. He called me Maggot, told me I whispered in the ears of young men, and they killed themselves in hostels. Now I walked into people's houses and blew their heads off. I created wreckage and carnage wherever I went because I could not control my own life. Inflicted pain and sadness and destruction to others. As it yelled at me, I stepped backward, stepped on an area of the carpet where blood had pooled. Slipped, fell on my ass, crawled backward. His head exploded. I reached the hallway, leaned against the wall, gasping for breath, the voice followed me, called me Maggot.

Stand up!

Ran out of the house, the way I came.

The voice followed me outside, as I ran from the house. I wanted to run away from all this. I felt the yellow grass on my arms, I did not feel the pressure of other times I was near this house. Wondered if, because he was dead, his hold on this land was gone, his grip on the property was not absolute.

Stop! I heard the voice following me, screaming.

Looked back, imagined the grass all coming out of the ground. The dead yellow grass floating away from here, the house crumbling, the rotten wood giving way, the dirt crawling over top of the house. It looked now like a hill, a mound of dirt, the grass was cleared, new grass grew, healthy green grass on the soil where the house used to be. Vegetables grew, fruit grew, things that gave life, that supported life. A giant tree extended to the sky, the earth waited for that man to die so it could grow again, so it could live again. It was a part of the world, not sectioned off vying for survival. Trying to stay alive.

The image disappeared, the yellow grass was back, the sad house was back, I felt this place changing already. Felt it moving away from what it once was. The voice whispered to me again. Always there, always over my left shoulder. I was able to ignore it. The voice was going on non-stop about my exploits. We had been away from each other, we needed to catch up.

I ran away from the house, ran to the beach, to my beach. I was trying to get away from the voice, but it kept pace with me. I was on the beach before I noticed I was holding the note in my hand. The final thought that the big man wanted to convey. I stopped running, even the voice stopped talking. I unfolded the note, it said: *I am sorry about Francis, it was not his fault.* What the hell did that mean? I took my shirt off, placed the note under a rock so it will not fly away. Ran into the ocean, wondering if he meant me, if he knew I was involved in the last few hours of Francis' life? But how could he know if I did not even know? Naturally, the voice had some answers for me. Tried to push it away but it seemed to have gotten stronger in its absence, more resilient to how I dealt with it before. I just tried to think over it. The salt water of the ocean had little effect on me, I got no strength from it. Dried in the sun, put my clothes on, carried the note with me while I walked back to town.

I phoned the officer and told him about the Leifhead house. Got a small bag from my apartment. Another note, I took it upstairs. Walked over to the hostel, sat on the bed in the room where Francis shot himself. Lay down on the bed, whispered to the room, "You probably already know this, but your father is dead. He killed himself in the same manner you did. He left a note, he wanted me to tell you that it was not your fault. He is sorry. He wants you to rest now. He knows that what he has done is wrong. He wants you to go now in peace." I waited for some kind of sign that someone or something heard me but I only heard silence. I waited on the bed for a while. Knew it had been a while because it was dark outside now. Sat up, took off the shirt I borrowed from Francis. Hung it up in the closet. Locked the door behind me. Walked down to the desk in the front foyer. I saw Marshall, gave him the key. Nodded at him, smiled, told him I would be back. He nodded at me, there was some kind of understanding between Marshall and me.

At my apartment, someone was waiting, standing, blocking the door. Helen had her arms crossed, she was watching me, she did not look impressed. I stopped three feet away from her, there was a distance between us, I did not want this distance, this gap. I opened my mouth, heard the words in my head, felt them, saw them but I made no sound. I only let out air, my shoulders dropped, my body dropped. I looked at this woman, someone I had dreamed about, someone who seemed to have infinite patience with someone like me. Someone who wanted to know me better, asked to know me better.

When you leave a hospital, when you go out into the world, the small space you inhabited becomes so much bigger and what you were satisfied with ten minutes ago was never enough.

I wanted to tell her everything all over again like she knew nothing. Her eyes were not judgmental, her ears that just listened, her mouth, her voice that told you what she thought but in a way that helped, in a way that you felt like a person. I wanted to be in her arms again, wanted to tell her about the Leifhead house, the voice that was back, that spoke right now, commenting on her, telling me what it thought she was thinking. Helen would take care of me, wanted to be with me, did not care what my situation was, what my problem was, she just wanted me.

I stepped closer to the car, stepped closer to her. She took my hand, her hand moved up my arm, she wrapped that arm around me, she wrapped the other arm around me, pulled me into her body. She pulled away from me, kissed me. She opened her mouth, I opened my mouth. We stood there for a long time. I finally pulled away, opened my eyes to her smiling at me.

That was when I backed away. I had to. I had no choice. We watched each other. I felt she saw behind my eyes, into my mind, into my heart. I blinked without seeing. I took another step back, another. I turned and walked into the night.

Chapter Ten

I didn't know where I was going. I just couldn't stay there with Helen, standing across from her acceptance, her ability to want to love me unconditionally. I backed away, unsure of where my feet took me, but going all the same.

I found myself in the same place as that first day I arrived in Greymouth. I poked between the two buildings and in the dark found the path that led to the beach.

As I walked through the pathway, stepping over the exposed roots and got closer to the clearing through the trees, I realized I was no longer in Greymouth.

That's when the lights in the distance turned on to illuminate the giant statue. The giant statue sat up on a hill near a residential area. The statue was built in the 1960s when the town mayor became obsessed with creating more culture in the area and thus commissioned several public art pieces. I remembered being a child and looking through my bedroom window at the lightbulb-infused statue, not sure what it was, but using it to stare at while waiting for my sister to return home from the pizzeria.

So many things happened here along this stretch of road. I stepped out of the Greymouth pathway and on to my old street. The houses looked smaller than I remembered, the houses closer together. I tried to see in windows, but most of them were dark, people were sleeping. I made it to the end of the street. Our house was the smallest, it was set up on a slight hill away from the other homes like we were embarrassed. There were no cars in the driveway, no lights on. It did not look like anyone lived here. I stopped at the foot of the driveway, stepped on the concrete. It was quiet on the street, but there was an influx of white noise. Felt a new found awareness. Felt every blade of yellow grass on the lawn, it seemed to bend, arch in my direction. I looked at the house, the house seemed to have grown a face. The house was looking at me, wondering what I was doing back. The air had become thick, I stepped through it, like stepping through water. I leaned down, looked in the window, cupped my hands around my eyes, saw familiar furniture, our old furniture. The house looked the same, this confused the hell out of me. I half expected that this house did not even exist anymore or maybe it never existed. I walked around to the backyard, it was the same but rundown. There had not been any upkeep, the grass was yellow, the cement steps cracked. I sat down on one of the steps, replayed what had happened here.

I thought back to when I lost control, if I ever had control. The air continued to get thicker, it was more difficult to exhale. Looked to the sky, there were lights from an airplane. I thought of all the different modes of transportation I had taken since I left here, since the hospital. The air closed in around my head. I wanted this to all go away, but I did not want to forget any of it. I did not want to throw it away, I understood it was a part of me, but I just wanted it gone, wanted it to stay in the past, stop popping back up in my life, just stop. I imagined there was something much more potent than my In Box and Out Box.

I imagined that instead of me travelling around on those planes and trains and buses, I imagined a past where a person looked like me and spoke like me but who was made up of memories. This past person was a shell that was no longer creating new memories. I had cloned myself, put all of the things I did not want inside this shell. I drove it to the airport, walked with it to the gate, hugged it, smiled at it. I said take care of yourself. It did not want to leave. It started pulling photographs out of its pockets, showing me different images, showing me what happened here in this backyard with the cat, showing another photograph of me in the bathtub, another with the police. I politely smiled, nodded my head, took its arm by the forearm, I pushed the hand with the photographs back into its pockets, turned it around, shoved it towards the gate. They took its ticket, it walked confusingly down the ramp. I watched, waved, I was rejecting these memories, they would always be there. I would always be able to conjure them up when I needed them or wanted them. I just did not need or want them any more right now. I sent them away on a plane, did not look at the destination, did not want to know.

I tried the back door of the house, locked. Went to the side window, the window was never locked. I snuck in through this window many times. I had filled out since then, it was harder to squeeze through. I fell down to the floor. Inside I saw two policemen walking towards me. I crawled backward until my back hit the wall. They walked past me, they were never there. I shook my head, stood up, let out a fart, the fart felt good. Walked through the rooms, they each had their own memories, the rooms each had their own feelings. I sent all those memories and feelings away on separate flights.

Walked upstairs, the air was thinning out, the thoughts bouncing around in my head slowed down. The voice over my shoulder had woken up, spoke to me low at first but I wanted it to talk, wanted it to see these rooms. I first stopped in my bedroom, saw myself ten years ago laying on the bed unable to get up. I wanted to sit down on the bed next to this kid, tell him it was alright, that everything seemed upside down right now but it would get better, that you needed to speak to your heart, listen to what it said. I would sit and ask the boy questions, ask what he was thinking. I would listen without judgment, put my hand on his hand, pat the hand, tell the boy after listening to him that it was okay to think these thoughts, to see things, to hear people talking over your left shoulder. I would tell him that he needs to find people to talk to, real people. He needed to speak with his sister, tell her something was wrong, that he needed help. I would say to him to get out of bed. It was so hard sometimes, but I would tell him to use all of his strength to get out of bed.

The voice over my left shoulder told me I could never go back. I said to it that I knew, I was not regretting anything, I was just showing you and myself how I had changed, so screw off, let me have this, and maybe you will go away. I left the bedroom, walked down the hallway, pushed open the door to the bathroom. It was precisely the same, nothing had changed. I saw flashes of blood, but I controlled them. Every time I saw one of these flashes, I pocketed it, packaged it, sent it away. I sat on the toilet seat, looked around, felt myself getting stronger. This was not as bad as I thought it was going to be, although I was still not getting any answers. The ones that I was looking for at least. I took my shoes off, took my clothes off. Ran a bath, there was still hot water. Filled the tub, got in the tub, scrubbed my body. Cleaned all the dirt off. Rested my head against the top of the tub, closed my eyes. Saw myself trying to hurt myself, trying to take the pain away, saw my brother seeing me in this position, saw the police, saw all the details of the night when everything changed.

My thoughts flashed back to Francis Leifhead. I thought about those lost hours. I had narrowed it down to five hours that were lost. Five hours when I was in town and Francis was still alive. I tried to construct them in my mind. I arrived in town - what happened? I pushed my brain hard, could not think. Wait, I remembered the spider web. Something was coming to me. The first hour I was in my apartment. Maybe I was making it up, but I could not fool my mind anymore the way I used to. The voice over my shoulder contradicted me, I told the voice to shut up. I had one hour accounted for.

Got out of the tub, looked in the cabinet. There was some old shaving cream, a razor. I trimmed my beard, shaved it off, crudely cut my hair. I was looking better, I turned towards the tub, shrugged my shoulders. Got dressed, walked out the front door, walked down the driveway, did not look back. The house was gone, it held no more memories. I sent it away on a train to a place I did not know.

Walked and walked, lost sight of my destination, lost sight of how to move forward. Where was I going? Why was I here looking in places that I worked so hard to get away from? Places I never thought I would return to? I walked back through rows of houses, saw no lights, no people. I wondered if anyone lived here. The sky was deep darkness. Followed the stars, the stars led me away from the houses, back to the highway. I walked along the road, every once in a while a car sped past me.

I found the exit, walked down the long country road, passed a sign that read Hugh's Centre for Recovery. It was a modest sign, large cement blocks with the letters etched into the side. Wondered who it was that made this sign, that sat painstakingly, chipping away a piece at a time. I kicked stones around on the gravel road, lights appeared from behind me. I jumped off the road, moved quickly across the long grass, crouched down. The lights passed. I could not see inside the car, decided to keep walking in the grass. Stepped parallel to the road. If I looked back, it seemed to go on forever, it seemed I could just keep walking and never get anywhere, never arrive, never have someone waiting on the other side happy to see me, ready to put their arms around me.

The voice over my left shoulder crept up on me. It was as though it grew in strength the closer we came to the hospital. The stars pressed down on me, took me back to my time out in the woods, outside of the hospital, reaching up, trying to touch the stars, imagining they were just out of reach, wondering if anyone else was looking at them the way I was. Sat down in the grass, hugged my legs close to my body, rocked back and forth. The voice over my shoulder threw in its comments, telling me I was making the right decision to come back to the hospital. I was not here to stay, just here to see, to put things to rest, to maybe put the voice to rest. It cackled, I pushed it away from me. In some ways I wanted to step on this road, have it go nowhere, I just wanted to keep walking, suspended in time, my only companion the scratching of the gravel below my feet, the stars, the rays of the sun, nothing else. I kept walking past the hospital, clear around the world, walking, always walking, never stopping, never knowing anyone, never getting close enough to someone to understand the concept of loss, losing myself in the goal of moving forward towards something I would never be able to find, and so I would never be disappointed.

I threw those ideas away in the Outbox, stood up, saw the lights of the hospital in the distance. Wanted to get through this, wanted to continue the life I had begun in other places, wanted to experience loss if that was what was in the cards. It was better than walking towards nothing, moving in the direction of the unknown, never knowing what was at the end if anything at all.

Helen popped into my head. The thought became concrete, formed entirely as though she was standing in front of me. I could almost reach out and touch her, ask questions about what secrets the ocean had told her. When I stepped forward, she stepped backward. She turned around, her back facing me, she led me, wanted me to make it, get this over with, not only get this over with but experience it, allow it to enter my body, take it for what it was, move on, face it.

As I got closer to the hospital, the lights got brighter,

and the image of Helen started to fade, she became translucent like a hologram until she was almost gone. She turned around, as she turned around, I closed my eyes, begged her to smile, just show me a smile. If she gave me a smile, I would be able to do this, I would be able to get through it. I opened my eyes, she faced me, she smiled, she read my mind and then she disappeared altogether.

I had arrived at the hospital. Stood at the border of the parking lot. Took stock of my situation. I did not think of how I was going to sneak back into the hospital. It seemed so easy when I sneaked out, but that was after a lot of planning. Now I stood there with about thirty seconds of time before someone noticed the strange man standing outside. I just decided to walk in like I belonged even though I no longer did belong. I headed to the front door, let out a fart before I stepped inside. The automatic doors slid open, inviting me in.

The air was different inside, the air reeked of familiarity. The same guard sat at his station reading a magazine. Surprising myself, I walked right up to him. He looked at me, I told him I was here to see the doctor. He nodded to the waiting room around the corner. I walked past the guard station, saw the monitors spread out before him. He went back to reading, I walked past the waiting room down the hallway.

I entered the stairwell, first visited the seating area in front of the window. Wondered if Margaret would be there waiting for me patiently, smiling as she saw me. I would tell her all about New Zealand, that it was more beautiful than any images conjured in my head. She was not there, so I went looking for her. I never even knew which room was hers. I looked in the small windows in the doors, I saw a lot of sleeping people, some were up looking through the windows outside to places they would never visit.

I found Margaret's room, saw her sleeping. The light from the moon illuminated her face. I tried the door, the door was open. Quietly stepped inside, padded lightly over to her bed, knelt beside her. She seemed to know I was here, she opened her eyes. Her eyes looked more tired then they did before. She whispered through her smile, "You came back to tell me what you have seen." She sat up in her bed. I smiled, nodded my head, she continued, "It is wonderful, isn't it?" She looked at me with hopeful eyes. I told her about the mountains, ocean, trains, ferries, the beach that were all mine. Told her every small detail. She was quiet, tears formed in her eyes, her tears rolled down her cheeks. She took my hand, lay back down in her bed. I said, "I wanted to thank you. I wanted to tell you everything because I wanted to thank you." She said, "I can see it in my mind, I can see everything. I am there right now." I told her she could go, that being there was so much more powerful and that just by going she would find the strength to get better. She shook her head, she said, "It is too late for me." I refused to accept this. She patted my hand, she said, "I appreciate you travelling all the way back here just to tell me, but you must leave. You must go back. You don't want to get stuck here again."

She saw the difference in my face, she felt the change in my voice. I must continue to change, to grow, I must leave, go back. She rolled over on her side, I whispered once more to her, "Thank you." She said quietly, "No, thank you."

I left her room, moved up one floor to my old level. A hallway I travelled many different times. I thought of all the kiwis I ate, how each one was my last, how I convinced myself every day that I was never going to enjoy another kiwi again. I tasted them, felt them travel down my throat putting nutrients into my insides, twisting around in my stomach. My mouth watered in the dark hallway. I reached my room, looked in the window through the door. Someone was sleeping in my bed. I looked to the other side, Jimmy was gone. Out with the old, in with the new. I guessed there was always someone who needed a bed. I twisted the doorknob, made no noise as I slipped into the room. Closed the door behind me, the man in Jimmy's bed was a young man, thin, his breathing laboured. Walked to my old bed, felt the power that this bed had over me.

The voice was back, the voice liked the bed. Memories returned, times where I kicked, scrounged for air, could not get out. The bed served as my island, I could not leave it. I seemed to sink into it, gasping. I remembered hearing the other voices of the hospital, the voice over my shoulder told me I should lay down, I should never get up, that I was weak, that was why I was here, I had returned because I could not make it, could not follow through with my plans. The voice told me the darkness was coming, a darkness that would take over again and I would never be able to get away from it. I tried to push the voice down, the voice was steady. The voice pulled power from the bed as I pulled power from the trees. It reminded me of Francis Leifhead. The voice told me I was directly responsible, that I had blood on my hands, that I should not be out among normal people. I tried to push it down, the voice was firm. I walked around the bed, looked at the man in the bed. He was curled up in the fetal position, his eyelids flickered, he was having a dream or a nightmare. I touched him on the shoulder, tried to calm him down. Looked at the bedside table, one of my New Zealand books sat open to a page about Greymouth. There was a photograph of the ocean view. I was brought back, wanted to return. I removed my hand from the man's shoulder, stepped away from the bed. The voice was pushing me, I turned away, looked out the window at the forest. There were tractors parked and unmoving. They had been cutting down trees, they were constructing a new building, replacing trees with concrete. I instantly slid to the ground, something deep inside snapped, came undone. I crawled to the wall, sat with my back against the window, tried to relax, tried to breathe. I pushed air inside my lungs, but it did not seem to get there. The darkness of the room got darker, the room thick with voices, not only the voice over my shoulder, others had joined in. The darkness crept up around me. I stuck my arm into the darkness, my arm disappeared. Pulled my arm back out. The darkness crept closer to me, surrounded me.

I was back in the darkness, but it was different this time. I was here by choice. Calmed myself, started at the top of my head, went through my mind, pushed everything down, it all went down. Moved through my neck, throat, into my shoulders. I checked them for any residue, found moments in my life that were long forgotten. I pushed those moments towards my heart. Felt my heart pumping blood, pumping more memories. The memories pushed down through my insides. I moved them all around, the memories travelled towards my pelvic area. I become slightly aroused, it did not last long. More memories. The memories moved first down my left leg all the way to my toes, then down my right leg. I wiggled my toes. My body was full of the darkness, I allowed it to enter. I felt a fart coming on, a big one, bigger than ever before. Held it in, wanted the darkness inside, kept it close, saw it for what it was. I moved it around, my eyes were open but saw nothing. The voice over my shoulder was here, it screamed, Yes! Yes! Yes! I allowed it to scream, I did not fight it, resisted nothing.

A thick rope was swung around my neck, the rope pulled tight. Someone pulled from inside the darkness, someone was pulling from behind me. In the dream, I habitually grabbed on to the rope at my neck, but this time I remembered what to do. I let go, dropped my arms to my sides, I did not fight. The rope got tighter still. I made no moves, my eyes were still open, I could not see who was pulling. The air squeezed out of my lungs, my throat closed shut. Finally, I grabbed the rope where it went off into the darkness, pulled the rope hard with more strength then I had ever had before. Summoned all the power I had ever gotten from touching trees and swimming in oceans and stepping on mountains. It was more strength than I realized, I had been building it up for a long time, building it up for this moment. A voice, my voice, screamed, PULL! My hands burned from the rope. Blood. I pulled hard, the rope started to come towards me, a hand emerged out of the darkness, it was pulling equally as hard, but I summoned more strength. I pulled harder than the hand, another hand appeared. It was losing this game of tug of war. A forearm appeared, another forearm, two feet popped out of the darkness, legs, the body of a person came out of the darkness like out of a cloud, like out of a dream. The person wore all black. A black hat was down over their face. I gave it one more heave. Pulled the person right up to me, merely inches away. The rope went slack, fell from around my neck. Gasped. Air sucked in through my mouth, my throat, flowed into my lungs, my heart thanked me. I told my heart, You're Welcome.

I knocked the hat off the person in front of me. Under the hat was Francis Leifhead. I realized at that moment, seeing this young man in person or in a dream or whatever this was, I realized I had never seen him before in my life. The remaining four hours of time I could not recall when I arrived in Greymouth come flooding back. I saw myself in the apartment, saw myself laying on the bed. I could not sleep, went into the main room, sat on the floor, got up from the floor, went for a walk, walked to the ocean. Remembered thinking that at night you could not see the water, could not see where it all led. The sea was a path into complete darkness. I sat on that beach for hours that night. I had nothing to do with Francis Leifhead, he was a troubled boy, he was like me in so many ways. He went in a direction I could have gone in. He chose his way, I had decided my way. I wanted him to stop forcing responsibility on me. Another realization came, one where Francis Leifhead had done nothing, it had all been in my head. I had to let go of responsibility. I could only control my own life, I had to leave him here. He smiled at me. I looked into his eyes, I saw what he was thinking. He thought that now he could have some peace, he could rest easier, he had no choice, but I had a choice. I smiled back at him, he patted me on the shoulder, looked down at the rope in his hand, his eyes apologetic.

The rope that was still around my neck pulled backward, yanked me off my feet. I looked up, Francis Leifhead was gone, someone approached me from behind, doubled the rope around my neck, took the other side, started walking, pulling me along the floor of the room, choking me. My arms grabbed at the rope around my neck. I felt it cutting into skin, it pulled me into the darkness, I was sucked through the window of the room and into dark clouds outside.

The rope pulled me through the black clouds farther into the darkness. I tore at the rope. I did not know what to do. Felt like I was going to die, that this was it. Was this actually a dream or something that was really happening? I heard mumbling from the person pulling the rope, I made out a word, the word was Maggot. I stopped moving, I let the person pull me along, choke me to death if that was what it wanted. I realized the voice over my shoulder had not said anything since I fell into the darkness. I concentrated all that I could on the thing pulling me. I heard Maggot, it was the voice that was usually over my shoulder. It stopped pulling me, the rope went slack for a moment, I gasped for air, the rope became tight once again. The person pulled me, then grabbed me under the arms, threw me into a hole that was even darker and more black than where I was before. I fell through the air until I ran out of rope. The rope snapped back, I felt my neck crack, it felt like my head was almost torn off. The rope choked me again, swung me back and forth.

I was in a small space, felt the walls all around me. The walls were slimy, the walls were cold. I slowed down the swinging, looked down, saw only darkness. Looked up, saw an opening slightly less dark than below. It was a well. I was still choking, I grabbed the rope, tried to pull it, the rope only got tighter. Heard the mumbling from above. Heard the word Maggot. I stopped struggling, went limp, slightly swung back and forth. I was dying, this was where it all ended. I was just a puppet on the end of a thick string that someone else had been pulling for all these years, obedient. Felt the oxygen leaving my body, my heart slowing down, the machine breaking down, the flow of blood slowing down, it was trying to tell my mind something. My mind was not listening anymore, the connection had been broken, the workers had all gone home, they had given up on me, I had given up on myself.

I started thinking about my daily kiwi. From this thought, I thought of other moments in my life that I appreciated, where I felt I had really lived, really taken that moment for everything it had to offer to me. Thought of Helen, Marshall, Margaret, my sister, Jimmy, the other Helen, I thought of people that I had really connected to and people where I had felt something strange, a new feeling, one where I felt loved.

Swinging on the end of that rope, I cried. The tears streamed down my face. At first, I thought they were tears of sadness, tears of loss, but as they fell, the tears told me a different story. The tears told me that they were happy tears, that each one of them held a piece of the people who had loved me and who I had loved. Each one contained a memory that was escaping from me, it wanted to get out because these memories wished to live on and they could not live on in a body that had decided to die.

A tingling sensation started in my fingers, a feeling of electricity. The excitement started moving around, generating more electricity, more power, it told me something new, something I desperately needed to listen to. It told me to hold on to those tears, do not let them go, grab them, hold them close, learn from them, aspire to experience that level of happiness once again.

The feeling in my fingers spread.

The electricity told me of the moments in my life, it explained how all the years were broken down into months, broken down into days, broken down into hours, minutes, seconds, each second into smaller and smaller increments. I only had so many of these moments, and the sum of my life added to how I had used each of them. The feeling started to become recognizable, started to become something new, something I had not felt often. Something called hope. The sense told me more about these moments, it said if I took each of these moments, used them in the right way, they multiplied. The moments got bigger, stronger. Hope grew. So when I finally reached my last days, I would have built up such a reservoir of hope that on my final moment, I would see that I had lived a life full of hope, I would smile, close my eyes knowing that I did my best with each moment. I had built up moments of insecurity, insanity, delusions, paranoia but since I left the hospital, other moments had presented themselves, other moments had been created, had been lived to the fullest. I had changed, I had been building the hope moments without even knowing it.

Mumbling from above, I heard the word Maggot. The energy in my fingers spread, the power ran throughout my body. The energy grew strong, it was fast, pushed out the darkness I allowed in from before. The darkness left my body through a series of smelly farts. I almost gagged, the darkness excited through my ears and nostrils, it reached my eyes, my eyes opened.

I saw this for what it was.

I lifted my arms over my head, grabbed on to the rope, pulled myself up. Placed my feet against the slimy wall, I walked up the side of the wall using the rope. Getting closer to the top, I moved slow hand over hand one step at a time. I saw the slightly less dark opening as I got closer. The person above was not ready to give up yet, they gave me slack which made me lose my balance. I fell down a few feet, my hands scrambled to grab hold of something along the wall. I only felt slime, there was nothing to hold on to. The person above grabbed the rope, the rope tightened, strangling me once again.

There was a cackling from above, mumbling, the word Maggot. The tingling was still in my fingertips, it was still pulsing through my body. I grabbed the rope, once again I could breathe, once again I continued climbing. The rope slackened again, I was ready this time. I spread my legs, lodged them, so each one pressed against the wall, the rope fell in my lap. A tremor of fear slid through me as the end of the rope fell past my face. I looked up, I was now suspended in the well only by my feet, the person above had completely let go of the rope. There was nothing to keep me here, I heard more laughter, the word Maggot.

I stayed still, wondered what to do. I could just remove my feet from the sides, fall into the darkness below. I wondered where it led if it went anywhere. Maybe it did not go anywhere, perhaps I would just drop forever? The tingling said no, the tingling talked, *Climb up! Go forward! Face this person, you know who it is, go after him.* I slid one foot upwards, pushed the other foot upwards, an inch at a time. I got closer to the top, slipped at one point, my heart seemed to fall down into my stomach. I steadied myself, brought my heart up to where it should be. An inch at a time and I was almost there. I could practically pop my head out the top of the well. I took one last jump from my feet, sprung up, used my strength, almost used it all up, and I was flying through the air. I grabbed on to the edge of the well, hanging from my fingertips, feet dangling below me. I held on tight for a moment, gave my legs a well-deserved rest. Two hands grabbed on to my hands, I looked up, I was staring into a face that had no features. Empty. He spat on me, called me Maggot. His voice was the voice that was usually over my left shoulder. One at a time, he peeled my fingers from the ledge. He lifted the pinky finger from my right hand, it fell down to my side, I was only holding on with my left hand. My entire body dangled, threatening to fall into the darkness below me. He started on my left hand a finger at a time. The breath left my body. I looked at him, looked into his eyes. I did not know what he wanted with me. To get rid of this person, to get rid of this voice, I had to bury it in my dreams. I reached my free hand up, grabbed hold of his wrist and with the rest of my strength and my power and electricity I pulled him into the well. His head banged on the other side, he fell into the black hole of the well, I heard no screaming, all I heard was Maaaaagggggggggggggoooooooooootttttttttt!

I hoisted myself up out of the well, looked around

me. There was still darkness, I did not see the light, but I felt a light inside of me. It burned bright, felt there was room inside now for this kind of light. What do I do now that I had taken the rope from around my neck? I turned back towards the well, leaned over the side, looked down into the black hole. A thought occurred to me, the idea was not full of electricity, it was only a thought, something that had popped in my head before, the thought told me I had to let go, the thought told me I had to sometimes give it all up in order to actually get out from this darkness. I looked around me one more time, it seemed the only way out of here was down the well. I stood on the edge of the well, thought about the fear, but I did not feel the fear. Let out a fart, it felt good, I felt all the air escaping out my ass.

I only had one choice, there was only one way out of here, one way back to where I started. I put my arms over my head, straightened up into the air like I was an Olympic diver. I jumped head first into the opening of the well, the noise was like a missile being launched. I flew through the air, went faster the more I flew, the darkness became darker. I floated, put my arms in front of my face like I was flying. The well went on forever, a sliver of fear slid through me, wondering if the well continued on indefinitely, that I would be dumped out the other side of the earth without a thought, but that fear went away. I just tried to enjoy the ride. This was like one big moment, the biggest of my life and I would land as a new person with my own voice in my head, not someone or something else.

In the distance a dim light became visible. I felt how fast I was going in relation to the light, the light reminded me of the one I saw in the lake, reminded me of the one I saw in the Leifhead house. I sped towards the light, was ready for it, prepared to see it for what it was. I had looked into the darkness, jumped head first into it, was this my reward? The tunnel got brighter, my eyes started to hurt, I got closer to the light, the light began touching my skin. I sped right into it, was surrounded by it, transported back.

I woke up in my old hospital room.

A voice, a different voice said, "Who in the hell are you and what are you doing in my room?" I shook the dream off, my neck hurt, my back ached from leaning against the wall. My eyes flicked open, blinked rapidly, my eyes tried to take in my surroundings. I was back in my old hospital room, the man sleeping in my old bed was sitting up, he looked at me, his forehead all scrunched up, he had a look of alarm on his face, repeated himself, "What the hell are you doing here?" I lifted my arms up in a harmless way. He thought it meant something else. He jumped at me, I stood up, backed away, got caught in the curtain separating the two beds. I struggled with it, he was pushing a button. I asked him not to, the light from the day poured in through the window, too many things were happening.

A nurse appeared at the doorway, it took me a moment to recognize Helen. She had cut her hair short, she had a look of surprise, I said, "I like your hair." She smiled, then remembered the situation. She told me I had to get out of here, I nodded. I looked around the room, three orderlies appeared at the door, I did not know any of them. There always was a high turn over rate for orderlies. They stepped towards me, the man in the bed was shouting, I told him to calm down. The man in the other bed started shouting, so I started shouting. I looked around, grabbed a steel chair in front of a desk, picked it up in both hands, slammed it against the window, it left a small crack. I slammed it again, another crack. I used all my strength, slammed the chair again, the window shattered, glass poured into the room with the sunlight. Helen said, "Wait! He is dangerous." I hoped she was saying that to stall them. I hoped she did not believe it. I would like to sit down, have a cup of tea with Helen, tell her about my adventures, tell her about the other Helen. I dropped the chair, took one look at the orderlies, looked at the ground below.

There were tractors, and construction workers cutting down trees. All had stopped, looked at the source of the noise. I looked back at Helen, at the orderlies, shouted, "Why are they cutting the trees down?" Their confusion was not my point, but I guessed it was a good thing. Helen said, "They're expanding the hospital." I shook my head, said, "Why can't they do it in the opposite direction where they've already cleared the trees?" They had no answer for this, I said this to confuse them.

I put one hand on the ledge, there were shards of glass. I cut my hand, it was not a bad cut. Hoisted my legs over the side, floated through the air to the ground below. I went with the fall. When I hit the ground, I rolled on to the grass, it was moist from the morning dew. I looked up to the window, the orderlies and Helen were looking out. I stood up slowly, gave them a salute which I thought was funny, but they were not laughing. I ran towards the construction workers, yelled at them, "Stop working! Stop cutting the trees down!" They all looked at me with more confusion, but I was serious this time. I did not have time to protest. The orderlies were already coming out of the hospital after me. I ran past the tractors, waving my arms shouting, "Stop! Stop!" They did not listen, I did not think they would stop. I ran past large piles of trees that had been cut down, I apologized to the trees on behalf of my fellow humans.

Now on my path, the path I walked on so many days. It felt good to be on this path. I touched the trees, felt their electricity pulsing through me. I veered off the path into the bush, it was the same area where I found Jimmy. I found his hiding spot, jumped down behind the bush and the trees. I looked through the trees at the path, the great thing about being pursued by orderlies was they wore white and could be spotted a hundred meters away in a forest. They continued on down the path, they did not see me. I lay here for a few minutes, slowed my breathing, let out some farts, closed my eyes. Felt the ground under me, the tree against my back, I heard some rustling to my left, I opened my eyes but did not move.

There was a small deer quietly walking towards me. It stopped a few feet away, took some leaves into its mouth, lifted its head to look at me, chewed on the leaves, stared at me. I wondered if it knew I would not hurt it? I guessed that was why it had come so close. I smiled at it, imagined it smiled back at me. It stepped closer, sniffed the air, walked by me, ran in the opposite direction.

I stood up, made my way through the trees. Tried to be as quiet as possible, tried not to step on bushes, plants. I did not want to disrupt the earth, did not want to hurt something that had given me so much strength. I continued to apologize under my breath to trees that might have had friends cut down by the construction men. I thought about the well, the darkness, Francis Leifhead, the man with the cackle. I shook my head, how utterly insane I would sound if I ever told anyone what was going on in my head.

I stuck to the woods, but I walked along the path, reached the lake. The lake was still here, it was not in my imagination. I was flooded with thoughts of when I was here at the hospital as a patient, how I got better when I made my own choices. Started from a lonely kiwi, ate my way to finding appreciation in the smallest swallow that led me out here into the woods to this lake and beyond. All of the things I had seen since the last time I was here. I sat in the bushes for a few minutes, staking out the lake making sure there was no one else around. Heard not a sound, not even the deer. Stepped out of the woods into the clearing that ran the length of the lake. Stopped, took it all in, breathed the air, allowed the sun to shine its rays on my face. Felt the power in those rays, I was low on strength after being down the well. Needed all I could get, there were no clouds in the sky, only blue that was deeper than the blue of the lake. I walked around the lake to the tree with the branches that spread out over the surface, the branches that I climbed up here when I fell in the water without knowing how to swim. Where I first saw the white light, the one at the end of the well that was not ready to show itself to me yet.

The tree stood tall beside me, touched it with my hand, it was warm. I thought about Francis Leifhead, remembered his smile. The rope had been removed from around my neck, the rope was not just let go of, but I fought to remove it, almost choked to death. I was proactive, grabbed life back from whatever was wanting it. I felt my responsibility to Francis was gone, it was absurd of me to think I played a role in his death, but my thinking pattern and the voice over my shoulder convinced me of anything. I did not feel there was any blood on my hands. Wondered if all this, everything, including me, standing beside this tree was another belief conjured from another personality, another voice in my head. The only one that had been in there since diving down the well was one that I agreed with that did not criticize me, it only saw things as they were and suggested moves that propelled me into the right directions. I wondered if I was close to peace, this elusive concept that I was learning more about every day. I had been absolved from any involvement surrounding the death of Francis Leifhead, exempted from the death of the faceless man in the well. I was merely throwing the voice away. The last thing was I wanted to be absolved from my own life. I had beaten myself up, criticized every move I had made, I wanted to be forgiven for my own mistakes, hoped it was not too late, wanted to forgive, maybe then I could move on, perhaps then I could find peace.

It was like the first time I climbed this tree. I steadied myself out on the branch, crawled out to the end right to the tip. Stopped, looked down into the water, saw the reflection of the sun. It looked like the bright white light. I saw the fish, the fish were floating, looked up at me, waved their gills, said, *Hello! You're back!* I smiled at my friends when I heard someone shout, "There he is!"

The orderlies popped out of the trees on the other side of the lake. I was a bit surprised, their arrival was not a part of my plans. I did not think anyone knew about this lake. The orderlies ran around, were already at the base of the tree, were yelling at me to come down. I just watched them from above. It was apparent I was not coming down. They discussed what to do. Finally one of the smaller orderlies started climbing. I turned to face the water, watched the reflection of the sun, looked back, the orderly was moving on to where the branch pushed out from the trunk. He straddled the branch, pulled himself towards me, I wanted to tell him that this branch probably could not hold both of us, but it was too late. I heard snapping, heard a big crunch. I apologized to the tree for hurting it, while in the air, I faced downwards, put my arms once again over my head like a diver, crashed into the water, making a small splash.

The water was warm for a moment, I stopped moving. Felt right to be here, like my entire life had led up to this point.

Remember this moment, allowed it to sink into my mind, body, insides, everything. I let the water settle, the fish scattered on impact, but they quickly return. They were all around me, deep in the depths of the lake. I saw the white light, wondered if it was just the sun piercing through the surface of the lake, but I saw that it was not coming from above, it was coming from below. The fish pointed towards it, I started swimming south, the fish guided me until I was close to it, and they departed as though they knew this was my moment, one that was only for me. I swam into the light, opened my mouth, expected water to fill my mouth, it did not, I could breathe. I extracted the oxygen from the water, it was here for me to have, I took it, breathed it in, felt the life it gave me, the darkness of the lake disappeared around me as the white light filled my field of vision. I reached the source of the light, it was nothing, the brightness did not seem to be coming from anywhere, it was just there, illuminating the darkest of places. I stopped swimming, floated in space, did not move my body, but it slowly moved around until I was horizontal to where I believed the surface to be.

Was this it? Was this all I had been looking for? I floated in the water, had come all this way, nothing had happened, I frustratingly floated as still as I could, wanting desperately for something to happen. The water became warm, it was hot on my skin like I was in a whirlpool or a hot spring or whatever it felt like to be in one of those two places. As I floated around in a circle, the warmness of the white light penetrated my skin, entered my body like reverse sweat, I felt it in every molecule. It was going into my insides reflecting against the inside of my skull.

I was taken somewhere else, back at the beginning. I was floating in another pool surrounded by water, there was a different kind of white light at the end of a tunnel, I was happy to be here, warm and not wanting to leave. The water got sucked out of the space I was in. I was sucked towards this new light. Two legs appeared on either side, I was sucked out of the space, the light was too bright, I cried. It was too painful, I wanted to go back into the tunnel. Someone picked me up, they placed me on a table. I saw my mother laying on a bed. She was passed out. A nurse picked me up, roughly covered me in a blanket. I was not happy to be here. I was placed in a place where I heard all kinds of voices, the voices were all around me. I tried to push them away. Even at this point, there was one voice that was louder than all the rest, but it was comforting. I listened to it, the voice was calming, sounded like it came from over my left shoulder.

After a long time, I was taken away by my mother

and father. I heard them arguing in the car. I cried, the voice over my left shoulder returned, made me feel good about myself. I met my sister, she had a smile on her face, she seemed happy to see me. I was delighted to see her, she played with me. I wanted to be around her all the time. My parents were not happy with me being around. My mother never nursed me although I would not have known this.

Since I was alone all the time, the voice kept me company, told me to do things I did not want to do. I did them anyways just to make it happy. They were little things at first like leaving a toy out where my father would surely step on it or pricking my finger with a pin. Since I understood that my parents did not want me around, I tried to make myself invisible. I was quiet, the only person that talked to me was the voice and my sister. I tried to make the two of them happy. This was what I remembered, that I always tried to make other people happy, that I gave in so quickly. The moments that made up my life were not my own but governed by others, mainly the voice.

My father left, the accident happened, my mother died. I fell into a state of only doing what the voice wanted. There was another form of memory that had been shielded from me by the voice. They were memories, thoughts that it did not want me to hear or to see. They were moments of happiness, moments of clarity. When I saw myself: who I was, what I was, where I was, not afraid, where I dealt with my problems, where I took control of myself, moved forward in building something from my life. This was the first time I had ever known I had those thoughts. They resembled a feeling that was opened up to me earlier in the well, the sense of hope, something I thought was new to me, something I never thought I learned. I was reliving so many things where there was a thick pane of glass surrounding me. I was breaking the glass, saw things for what they were. It was nothing special, I only knew what the voice told me, I believed in it like a religion, held a belief without asking any questions.

I was weak, but I grew strong.

This was the point where the voice usually had something to say, but it said nothing. It was not here, I felt a void where it used to be, played the images of my life across the inside of my skull. They flipped back and forth in time, I saw them without the voice, saw them as though I made all those decisions, I did all those actions, and then it hits me like nothing else in my life had ever hit me before. Through all this confusion, all this mash of images, I now knew that there never was any voice over my left shoulder. The voice was part of me all along, it was me. I never asked any questions about its existence because it had always been there. I assumed everyone had their own voice – they do have their own voice, but they understood that it was them. I made a separation. From the start I created a reason for me to do all of these things, to be able to shift responsibility to someone else so I would not have to deal with the results, I would never have to take the blame over my actions or my thoughts.

Rifled through all my memories, everything I could get to. I saw it all but from a different perspective. I witnessed all of these memories where the voice over my shoulder had something to say, had something to criticize. I did not hear the voice over my shoulder, I heard it inside my head, it was a part of me, it was me. I felt that to gain absolution I would have to forgive the voice, let it go, but underwater covered in white light I learned that it was me that I had to forgive. I had to see what I saw, I had to experience these moments in a new way, a way where it was me all along. I had to gain absolution from myself. I was sucked out of the moments of all the times I played along with the voice, played along with believing it was someone else, blaming something else. I was sucked into a different kind of womb, the one that was this moment, the moment that was happening right now where I made a choice to believe in something else. Discarded the voice over my left shoulder, forever left it down in that well with the slimy walls, never heard from it again because I had a new voice, one that was mine living inside my head, that directed me forwards instead of sideways, pulling me towards where I wanted to go, helping me to understand the concept of peace.

I was sucked back to the here and now. The white light was gone, the water grew cold, I choked on the water, it no longer gave me oxygen. The fish had returned, the fish looked scared, they did not even travel this far below into the darkness. The rays of the sun could not penetrate this far down, the fish told me something, they wanted me to live, they wanted me to head to the surface. Bubbles appeared from my mouth, they shot up in the direction of the surface, I followed the bubbles, I said to the fish, Thank you! I felt them pushing me up, up, up and I broke through the surface, sucked in air.

The orderly on land helped the one who fell into the water back on to shore. I was only down there for moments, but they were the most critical moments of my life. They were concerned with their own, they did not notice me yet. I turned in the opposite direction, swam faster than I ever had before. There was a new found strength in my muscles, I kicked and stroked without noise. Remembered swimming across this lake so many times. I was halfway across before someone noticed me. I made it to the other side, they were still running around the lake. I climbed out of the water, almost dry from the sun by the time I reached the path. I knew these woods like the back of my hand. They would never find me. I jumped into the woods, my footprints disappeared. I ran through the trees like they were opening up a path just for me. The trees were my friends, they wanted what I wanted. I stopped after ten minutes of running, looked behind me, there was no sign of the orderlies.

I moved slower now, was in no rush, these moments were now mine, I wanted to live inside each of them. I touched every tree I passed. Thanked them for its protection. I reached the end of the forest, the path opened up beyond the trees, and I was-

-thrust out on to the beach in Greymouth. I blinked at my beach, at the ocean, the sun was coming up over the horizon. Ran through the path and returned back to the town. Helen was at my front door, she turned around, looked at me. She came over, hugged me tightly. We held on to each other. My head was over her shoulder, facing towards my apartment door. The door was opened and in the hallway was my sister. She smiled at me, nodded her head, made a face of mock approval. Helen and I let go of each other. My sister stood before me, she put her hands on my shoulders, there were tears in her eyes. She hugged me, nobody had talked yet, there was so much to say, no one knew where to start, so we just all sat down in silence until a feeling started in my belly, moved through my insides, up my throat, came out of my mouth. I started laughing. For a moment, they just looked at me. I thought of stopping, but I did not care, this was a moment I wanted to remember forever, it was being etched into my brain as it happened. Soon Helen was laughing, she was bent over at the waist, she was laughing so hard. My sister was trying not to, but her smile betrayed her. She let out a big bellowing laugh that I had not heard very often, not since we were young.

We talked all night. We told Helen everything, understood that she was someone special, someone we could trust. The same with Marshall, who joined us after closing up the front desk. Helen knew a lot about my story, but I repeated it for Marshall, for my sister. My sister chuckled at choosing the name Paul

Dore. I even told them how I felt I was responsible for Francis Leifhead's death. Marshall and Helen said he was entirely on his own, I had nothing to do with it. Told them about going back to the hospital, told them about the white light so long ago, the one that I saw again in the Leifhead house. How I found him with his head blown off, how it prompted me to find that white light again. Told them about the ropes, the well, the man with the voice jumping into the well, waking up, almost being caught, breaking the window, running into the woods. I told them about the deer, about the orderlies finding me on the branch, falling into the water, floating towards the white light, being born again, finding things out about myself I never knew before, breaking through the surface, out-swimming them, running back through the woods. I told them how things had changed, how I could not wait to get back here to see Helen and what a surprise it was to find my sister. I knew they would get along.

We told stories to my sister into the night. Helen and Marshall were very generous in their opinion of me. They told her about the mountain climbing, she kept looking at me, shaking her head, slamming her hand on my knee, saying, "I can't believe it!" I sat back. I was so tired, but I could not leave, I never wanted this night to end. I wanted to sit here forever until the four of us knew everything about each other. Helen and Marshall told my sister everything about them, she complimented them on the hostel, on building their own business. They asked what she did, she smiled, said, "Maybe another time. There are so many other things to talk about." I was ready to pass out, my sister gave me another hug, told me she was staying for a week. She wanted to know my life here, wanted me to show her everything. She went upstairs to her room. Helen put her arms around me, held me tight, took my face in her hands, kissed me. I was instantly awake. She took me by the hand, walked back to my apartment, we went upstairs.

The next day I brought my sister around to all the places that were special to me in Greymouth. We visited the flower shop where they were so glad to see me, asking if I was coming back to work. I introduced my sister, they told her all about my talents with arranging and growing flowers. She smiled proudly at me. They had back orders for me to do. I needed a rest, they said whatever as long as I came back.

We walked to the beach. Up the small hill through the woods to the beach on the other side. The beach that felt like it was my beach. I told her this was where I met Helen. She sat down on the sand, I sat down beside her. We watched the waves go in, go out. I told her the water was warm. She was silent for a moment. She started laughing, she could not swim, never learned how. I told her it was easy, I taught myself. We stripped down to our underwear, stepped into the water, she said this water felt different. I told her it felt different because it was the ocean. We went in up to our waists, she stopped, told me she could not go further. I took her hand, said I was here for her, I would help her.

Something struck me at that point, I just started talking, told her things I never thought I would. I had explained what happened to me, but I did not tell her what I was thinking, feeling. I let it all out, I said, "You held my hand for so long. You supported me through all this. I was gone listening to another voice, lost to myself. You guided me from a distance, you gave me strength. I knew no matter how far I strayed something inside me, even if it was not conscious, knew that you were there pumping your fists at every little victory I achieved, no matter how small it was. When I was in the hospital, I started eating kiwis, I touched trees, I wiped everything out of my life, started at zero. I took everything away except you. I knew I could get rid of everything, but I could not wipe you from my memory. I held you close, you are the only person that has dealt with me in an understanding way without judgment, only support. I sometimes feel like I do not know you very well, that we have never been very close, but I feel that you are always with me. I can feel that I am in your thoughts all the time, which binds us closer than anything. I know that you have had to be strong for both of us, not only financially but in other ways. You made decisions in your life that maybe you did not want, perhaps you wanted different things, but you pushed those aside so you could get us both through this. I have seen you focus on me, but I want to tell you right here right now that I am pretty sure I am okay, and I am okay mostly because of you, and I want you to start looking at yourself, at what you need. I want you to take care of yourself or even let me take care of you. I do not know what all this means but I know that you have ignored yourself for so long, you have been so strong for so long that you have not been able to let go, not been able to lower your defences to put yourself first. You have always looked after me, always had me to deal with. I am so thankful that you were there, but I am better, I am almost there, and you can now look into yourself and do something you want.

"We were two people that everyone forgot about. I am okay with that. I heard voices, they told me what to do, I did them, I realize it was my voice all along. I wonder what that has to do with anything, I do not know, but I know that we all have some kind of deficiency, something wrong, sometimes we do not want to see it, want to ignore – even you, the strongest person I know has something. What you have to do is to let go a little, loosen up, let us both be strong together instead of only you because you have done your job, you have done it well. Look at us, we are both here when so many just wanted to forget about us. A large part has to do with you, but we have also done this together. We only have so many moments, I want you to start having your own moments, ones that are yours, ones that we can share together. I want to tell you that you have your brother back. I was lost for so long, you were running alongside me, trying to tell me which direction to go and I finally made the right decision. Here we are together, floating in the ocean, off the largest beach possible, during a beautiful day with the sun smiling down at us. This is our moment together, to realize we are brother and sister. We have made it, we are holding hands, our minds are intact, we are stronger than ever. Let me take you in my arms, let me help you swim, let me help you now. We can do it together, there is no end to what we can do together. You are my sister, the only family I have. I learned a new concept called peace, which I am still learning about. There is something else I want to tell you, an entirely different story, one where tears filled my eyes, and I realized that I am loved, and I love, and there is nothing we cannot do without this. We may fall, but we just get back up, we keep moving, we pick each other up but never forget that we are loved, and we love."

She leaned into my arms and let me help her swim in the ocean.

Chapter Eleven

That day my sister and I walked out of the ocean, we lay down on the beach, let ourselves dry in the sun. We raced along the beach, I watched my sister laugh, laughed with her. We walked out to the Leifhead house, stepped up on the porch, the feeling in the air changed like it re-started itself. There was a for sale sign out front. As soon as I saw it, I asked my sister for a loan but I told her it was only a loan, I would pay her back. We went right to the real estate office, we closed the deal that afternoon. I was given the keys to my new house.

We went around to my apartment, collected my few things, I introduced my sister to Margaret. She invited us in for tea, she couldn't get enough of my sister. I told Margaret I was moving out but only down the street. We told her to keep the rent that was paid until the end of the year. We entered the hostel, my sister went up to get her luggage, she travelled light just like me. I told Marshall and Helen that I bought the Leifhead house. This made Helen so happy, it was a commitment, it meant I was staying. I told her, of course, I was staying. She had her doubts, but deep down she knew it, she knew I was staying. She sprinted at me, jumped into my arms.

We went over to the house, opened it up with my keys, walked inside. A strange feeling started in my feet. The feeling was a tingling sensation, it travelled up my legs through my insides. It was the feeling of coming home, it was the feeling that after all this time of living in houses, apartments, hospital rooms that were never really mine, I had finally got my own house, a place I could call my home. We ran all around the house looking at everything. The furniture was still here, I expected to see the white light but knew it was not here. The only thing missing was the couch where he shot himself. I told my sister about it, how I found the body, that the head re-formed, spoke to me, prompted me to go back to the hospital.

We marvelled about how clean it was on the inside, but it needed work on the outside. There was a thin layer of dust on everything. The house had been neglected, but it had new owners now that would take good care of it.

That week we worked hard on that house. Cleaned the inside, got rid of unwanted furniture. We worked well together. There were periods of time where we did not talk, lost in our work, our thoughts. We cleared out all the yellow grass. We brought in new soil, planted grass that would grow strong. In the backyard, we took away all the garbage, old useless items. We made a space where we planted seeds. We planted vegetables, fruit, anything we could get our hands on. I wanted to become an expert gardener. Wanted to watch it grow like a father watching his son. Wanted to be proud of what sprouted out of the land knowing that I had a hand in creating it. That my sister and I did it together. Along the garden around the perimeter of the lot, we planted trees. Someday I wanted to look out the window and see only trees. It might take a while, might take years, but I had become a patient person. I would look every day out the window for when the trees come out to say hello. It might be like watching water boil, but I would be here, I would watch them push themselves up towards the sky. We repaired the back porch, the front porch, we sanded the old paint that was peeling away, we put on a new coat of paint than another. One we painted white, it seemed to be a different kind of white, one that sparkled, glowed, that could be seen for miles around.

People came from the town. They brought us food,

welcomed us, complimented us on all we had done in only a week. We told them there was nothing the two of us could not do together. My sister had to go, she had business, she would be back sooner than later, this was her home as much as mine. She planned on returning every month, maybe even more. She would keep working but wanted to slowly close out her business, pass it along to others. Her heart was not in it anymore, she had many other things she wanted to do. Helen and Marshall came by the house to say goodbye to my sister. She drove away from me down a different road, in a different way, we all waved to her. I felt her smiling at us. She stuck her arm out the window, waved back at us. I did not feel sad about her leaving because I knew she would be back and I knew she would be back to stay some day.

I continued working on the house myself. Woke up early every morning, went for a run by the beach, for a swim in the ocean, came back home, worked on the house. I finished the paint job, moved to the roof. I took all the old tiles off, replaced any holes that were rotting. I put on an entirely new roof myself. I worked shirtless every day, felt the sun beating down on my back. Every once in a while I stopped, just to look up, to drink the morning in, thank it for being here with me, sharing this moment with me. My body became fit, I took on a bronzy colour as I worked on my own roof, on my own house, building a home so it could be mine.

Every day, after I worked for an hour or two on the house, I went to the flower shop, learned more about flowers. How they grew, what the best environments were, which flowers grew best with each other. We took over the shop next door to expand the store because it got so busy. When the owner retired, we built a small greenhouse, grew our own flowers. People from all over came to buy them. My boss at the flower shop asked if I wanted to buy into the business. We shook hands, I was now involved in the day to day decisions that included more than just the flowers. I found a hidden talent that I was good with numbers, saved us money. Our business prospered.

I started writing small articles for the local newspaper. My work was widely read. I began writing articles for other publications. I liked to write, there was some kind of itch to tell my story. Maybe there was some worth in sharing my story? I jotted down notes when I could, perhaps I would write a book someday?

I finished the roof, changed all the windows. It looked like a new house, but it had still retained the original style. This was important to me, I wanted to keep a memory for Francis, wanted to keep his house recognizable just fixed up. I moved to the inside, redid the floors, painted the walls, knocked a wall down to make one giant room. I lay carpeting, renovated the kitchen.

Every day I visited the hostel on my way to work and brought Helen a single flower. Every night after I finished, I tried to have a different flower for her. My sister came to visit, she helped me finish the house. I let her paint her own room, I wanted her to be comfortable, provide every incentive I could find for her to come and visit.

When we finished, I went over to the hostel. I asked Helen if she wanted to come and live with me. She smiled, we packed up her things that day. She saw my sister, hugged her. Marshall came over, we made a huge dinner, the word spread around the town, everyone stopped by, there was a party happening. The residents brought food and wine, I gave them tours, we stood in the back, I pointed to the different vegetables, to where the trees would be. They admired my roof, told me they were happy I decided to stay.

At one point, I was outside alone, I looked through the windows of my house, looked into my home. I saw friends, saw loved ones, people I wanted to be around every day, who wanted me around, who were here not because they had any other reason except they wanted to. Helen came outside, she put her arms around me, she looked in the windows with me, she knew what I was thinking. I put my arm around her, I said, "Let's go inside."

My sister was in an in-depth conversation with a man that lived on the other side of town. His wife recently passed away in an accident, no one had been able to make him smile since then, but he had not stopped laughing since talking with my sister. She charmed him like she charmed everyone. They spoke all night, the next morning she told me she would be coming more often, she liked it here, it was a place she saw herself stay someday.

You could say my life after this was mundane, that it seemed like I did the same thing every day. I ran, swam, grew flowers, grew vegetables, but I did not see it as mundane. I would forever remember the kiwi and every night I went to bed smiling, looking forward to tomorrow, appreciating what I had right now, that I had the opportunity to be in control of tomorrow, but also knowing that something unexpected might happen. I watched my grass grow. We had a feast with the first batch of vegetables from our garden. I was there on the day the trees broke through the earth.

The voice was still there always, but I knew it was my voice only trying to tell me something. Instead of fighting it, I listened to it, empathized with it, tried to understand what it was telling me. I took my medications, went to the doctor regularly but as I got older, it would become rare that I had setbacks, mainly because I had learned how to deal with them. The way I looked at it was I chose the darkness for so long that I had no concept of anything else. What I saw in that white light was something else, a flip side, a different direction, something else to surround myself in. I discovered with the help of a few kiwis to take in every moment, to understand that it was there for you to experience, to do with what you wanted and I had my tomorrows back. I could look forward from this moment right now, I saw tomorrow, and I smiled, I only smiled because whatever the feeling was, I knew that I had taken responsibility for myself. I had those around me that I loved, I saw things for what they were, I had a different understanding of who I was, and I liked this person. I had looked very deep inside, and the result after everything was said and done was that I loved who I was now. This seemed like a simple concept, but I had always had problems with the simple things in life. It was more difficult then I thought, in some ways the hardest thing I had ever done. I was still learning, and what a great position to be in where I fully appreciated every moment while knowing I would learn something new about myself tomorrow. Everyone always talks about living for today, but tomorrow is more important. There were days where I never wanted to see tomorrow, there were days I never thought it would come but I love this simple concept of tomorrow. I even loved saying the word, the way it rolled out of my mind, dropped on to my tongue, pushed through my lips like a breath of fresh air and I said it to myself sometimes, just the word, just quietly to myself.

Tomorrow.

Acknowledgements

This book was written and re-written over many years. It was a long and arduous experience. It taught me a lot about myself, and showed how sometimes fiction can be closer to the truth than I would care to admit.

Wayson Choy has been a mentor and friend for many years. His inspiration can be found in every word I've written.

The Stories We Don't Tell community has been crucial to my development as a writer, performer, and person. Thank you Stefan Hostetter and Brianne Benness for letting me in on this ride with you both. Thank you to all the participants and the amazing audience members.

Thank you to my wonderful family: Chris, Shannon, Joshua, Austin, and Jaxson. The memory of my father still looms large and I hope he has found peace. Of course, to my number one fan: my lovely mother.

My love to you all.

About the Author

Paul Dore is the author of *The Walking Man*, which the Quill and Quire called: "A globetrotting tale that imagines new ways to get at what's really going on." He is a podcaster, blogger, creative consultant, and performer. Paul lives in Toronto with his two aloe plants, Peter and Mary.

To learn more, visit pauldore.com.